DISASTER STRIKES

Edited by Kathryn Cole
Cover and text designed by Tania Craan
Typeset by Susan Buck
Printed and bound in Canada by Friesens

Library and Archives Canada Cataloguing in Publication
Draper, Penny, 1957-, author
        Red River raging / Penny Draper.
(Disaster strikes ; 8)
Issued in print and electronic formats.
ISBN 978-1-55050-584-9 (pbk.).--ISBN 978-1-55050-585-6 (pdf).--
ISBN 978-1-55050-803-1 (epub).--ISBN 978-1-55050-804-8 (mobi)
        1. Floods--Red River Valley (Minn. and N.D.-Man.)--Juvenile
fiction. I. Title. II. Series: Draper, Penny, 1957- . Disaster strikes ; 8.

PS8607.R36R42 2014   jC813'.6   C2014-900457-5
                                              C2014-900458-3
Library of Congress Control Number 2014931276

2517 Victoria Avenue
Regina, Saskatchewan
Canada S4P 0T2
www.coteaubooks.com

10 9 8 7 6 5 4 3 2 1

Available in Canada from:
Publishers Group Canada
2440 Viking Way
Richmond, British Columbia
Canada V6V 1N2

Available in the US from:
Orca Book Publishers
www.orcabook.com
1-800-210-5277

Coteau Books gratefully acknowledges the financial support of its publishing program by: the Saskatchewan Arts Board, The Canada Council for the Arts, the Government of Canada through the Canada Book Fund and the Government of Saskatchewan through the Creative Industry Growth and Sustainability program of the Ministry of Parks, Culture and Sport.

To the resilient people of the Red River Valley

TABLE OF CONTENTS

My name is Finn Armstrong.
The weirdest thing happened to me.
This is the story.
Believe it or not.

CHAPTER 1

Exile

February 1997

If I close my eyes, I can almost see the pyramids. There's a camel too. I can see it lumbering along as it moves from one side of my eye to the other, just underneath my eyelid. Then the camel disappears from sight as it crosses my nose and reappears in the other eye. It's like I'm watching it through the lenses of a pair of glasses. Cool. I can feel the sun on my face, and the inside of my nose feels itchy from all that dry air. I'm in Egypt.

Not.

I'm actually sitting in Gran's kitchen. Stupid blue ducks on the wallpaper, cutesy ruffles on the curtains and sleet slashing at the windows. Fifteen below zero, but Gran keeps right on smiling. How can she be so cheerful? After only one day she's driving me crazy.

"Hot chocolate, Finn? It's a good day for it," she says, handing me a steaming mug. I want to tell her that it's not a good day for anything. That would be thanks to my parents, my wonderful, loving, brilliant, lying parents. The same parents who just wrecked my life.

They promised. They promised that I could go with them to Egypt.

You see, my parents are super smart, they're both "-olo-gists." My dad is an anthropologist, which means he studies people. My mom is cooler. She's a potamologist. And I think that's cool because I'm probably one of the few people in the world who even know what that is. For your information, a potamologist is a specialist in the study of rivers. In the winter my parents teach at the University of British Columbia in Vancouver, where we live, and in the summer we go all over the world to check out rivers. You get it? Mom studies rivers and Dad studies the way people live around rivers. They're a perfect team.

I'm part of the team too, not a real scientist yet, but almost. My job is to be the kid and I'm perfectly suited for it, since I actually am one. Ha ha. The deal is this: Dad hires one of his grad students to come with us, supposedly to be my babysitter. But I'm actually bait. The grad student's real job is to write a paper about how the local kids live. So they need me to get out there and play with all the kids. It's a rough life, but like they say, somebody's got to do it.

And it's no joke, you know. Try making new friends over and over again when half the time you don't even speak the same language. See? Luckily I'm small and kind of funny looking. (I take after my dad.) Most kids would rather laugh at me than beat me up. I'm okay with that because, well, who likes to get beat up? But all the time they're laughing at me, this is what I'm thinking inside my head: the bigger the bully, the smaller the brain. It's a fact.

This summer, we were going to Egypt to study the Nile River. I was going to ride a camel, see the pyramids and get up close and personal with a mummy. It's what we do – go where the rivers take us. It's even our family motto, *The Armstrongs Go With the Flow*. Beats summer camp, doesn't it?

Except my parents lied.

This is what happened. Two weeks after Christmas, Dad comes flying into the dining room waving this paper around in the air. He looks a little like a young Albert Einstein, just so you know, and when he goes crazy his hair makes him look kind of wild.

"Amanda! Amanda!" he shrieked. "We got it!"

Got what?

Mom was busy in the kitchen and didn't hear him at first. "What did you say, Andrew?" she called out. Dad just steamed past me, yelling the whole time.

"Russia came through! Finally, we're going to Russia!"

Russia?

It clearly meant something to Mom because she whirled around and I swear, she actually tossed the salad right up into the air. Honestly, she did. Then the two of them started doing this funky dance thing around the kitchen, and I still didn't know what was going on. So I had to yell.

"WHAT'S GOING ON?"

The looks on their faces were hilarious, almost as if I was the parent, and I'd caught them stealing cookies or something. I had to laugh.

"Finn, we need to talk."

I stopped laughing.

Turns out the application to go to some stupid river in the Russian Arctic had been in the works for eight long years. Which means they must have sent it in when I was in kindergarten. The town at the mouth of the river is closed to foreigners, and it's really hard to get permits, which is why it took so long.

"But the work they're doing in Dudinka with explosives to break up ice jams on rivers is unique. I've wanted to study it for years. And the local Ket people, well, there are only a thousand of them left in the world. You understand how important this is, Finn, don't you?"

Dudinka? You've got to be kidding me.

It's all a little hard to process. Instead of Egypt, my parents are going to Dudinka, a little Russian town north of the Arctic Circle on the Yenisei River. Instead of just being away for the summer the permit says they have to go right now. And instead of going with them, I am staying. There is no permit for me. (Yeah, because they think I'm five!) So I am off the team.

And that is a problem. What do you do with an almost fourteen-year-old boy halfway through the school year? Easy. You send him to Winnipeg in the dead of winter to live with two old people.

Mom and Dad said that Gran could be part of my new research team. "You know that research grants are hard to come by, Finn," said Mom. "You have to go with what comes. For us, that means Russia. For you, well, for all intents and purposes your grant application to go to Egypt has failed and you have to put your project on hold. All scientists have to deal with this sort of disappointment. We'll do Egypt next year. Look at this as a good chance to connect with your family and study your heritage. Make that your new research project."

Yeah sure, Mom. Which is cooler: studying old people in Winnipeg or camels in Egypt? Duh. This is nothing but a brush off. I know the truth.

I have been exiled.

I sip the hot chocolate. Gran's making chocolate peanut butter squares, my favourite. It's nothing more than a bribe and I'm a little smarter than that, thank you. Chocolate can't fix the fact that I'm sitting in Winnipeg in the middle of February while my parents fly off to the Russian Arctic without me. Actually, it's worse than that. I'm not even in Winnipeg. I'm in this tiny village called Ste. Agathe, someplace out in the boondocks, way south of Winnipeg. I mean, there is nothing here, unless you count the cartoon cows and chickens and ducks on the wallpaper. The kitchen clock is a pig face and the piggy eyes roll back and forth as the seconds tick. I can't even look at it.

Gran doesn't live alone. My great-grandfather lives here, too. It's really his house, although I'm betting the ducks are Gran's idea. Just so you get the family straight, Great-grandfather had a son who married Gran, only the son died a long time ago. They had a son (before Gran's husband died, obviously) and that's my dad. My dad had a son and that's me. My great-grandfather likes to be called Armstrong, which is actually our last name, because he says calling him Great-grandfather makes him seem old. Yeah, well, he *is* old, probably the oldest person in the universe, and he totally freaks me out. Right at this moment, the old man is sitting on a stool in the corner of the kitchen staring at me. He kind of looks like a garden gnome, only mean. He hasn't said a word since I arrived.

"Hi." I say it kind of loud, just to be sure he can hear.

"You don't have to shout. I'm not deaf, nor am I an idiot."

Okaaay.

"Be nice, Armstrong," Gran says quietly.

"Why should I? Andrew was the one who decided to leave the farm. Andrew was the one who decided to have a kid then dump him. Why do I have to deal with the fallout?"

Great. So now I'm fallout. I've been called a lot of names before but never nuclear waste.

"Armstrong! Why don't you go out to the barn? I'll call you for lunch."

Armstrong pushes himself off the stool and goes to the little mudroom off the kitchen. He takes a heavy coat and hat off a hook, then glares at me one last time before trudging out into the storm, slamming the door behind him.

Things just get better and better. Newsflash, old man: I don't like this either, not that anybody ever cares what I think.

"Finn, please don't mind him. He's angry, but not with you. He's angry with life in general and there's nothing either you or I can do about it. We're going to have a fine time together and, if need be, we'll just ignore him, okay?"

No. It is absolutely not okay. I am not prepared to have "a fine time" with my grandmother. I have money. There are buses. I can get myself back to Vancouver, which isn't Egypt but at least it isn't this.

Gran tries to change the subject. "On Monday I'll drive you to Easthaven to register you for school. Easthaven Collegiate is a great school and I'm sure you'll like it."

Oh, sure I will. Breaking in a new school halfway through the year is pretty much the last straw. "Easthaven? Not Ste. Agathe?"

"No, the school here is French. If you want to go to English school, you need to take the bus to Easthaven. Don't worry, it's not far. The school bus will pick you up at the end of the lane."

"Gran, forget school. I'm already set up for homeschooling. I'll just do that." That was for the Egypt trip, the one that isn't happening. Maybe I can get something out of this disaster, like no school.

"Your mom and I talked about that, Finn. She wants you to meet some friends because you'll be here at least until fall, maybe longer. School's the best way to do that."

Yeah, right. Adults truly have this romantic idea of school the way it was back when they were kids. Now high school is a war zone. It's survival of the fittest, to quote one of my favourite scientists.

I'm closing my eyes again. Maybe the camel will come back. Exile sucks.

CHAPTER 2

Easthaven Collegiate

I spend the weekend ignoring them both. By Monday I'm so bored with old people that I'm almost looking forward to school. On the way there, I decide to ask Gran why Armstrong is so mean.

Gran sighs. "What's your last name, Finn?"

Huh? What does that have to do with anything? "Armstrong."

"Armstrong. Strong arm. It's your name, your father's name, and your great-grandfather's name. Your great-grandfather has always been proud of that name and proud that he was strong enough to live up to it."

So why are we all so scrawny? I think to myself.

"You know that the Armstrong family has farmed this land for generations?"

"Not really."

Gran chuckles. "Your dad is so busy studying other people that he's clearly neglected studying his own. The Armstrongs came from Scotland and were among the earliest settlers in the Red River Valley. We've been here since the early 1800s. Life was very hard at first and many settlers gave up and left. Not the

Scots. They stayed. They worked the land and handed it down, from generation to generation. But for the Armstrong farm, it all ends with your great-grandfather. His own son died." Gran sighs at that. "And his grandson, your dad, isn't interested in the farm. Armstrong feels that he has failed."

"But it's not his fault that Dad decided to go away and become a professor. It's not like Dad's a bum or anything."

"No. In Armstrong's mind, the failure is that he didn't instill enough pride in the family heritage to make your dad want to stay."

Huh. Talk about living in the dark ages. That kind of father/son pass-your-profession-down-the-line thing went out ages ago.

Gran is turning into the parking lot of Easthaven Collegiate. "Here's your mom's paperwork. They probably won't get you on the bus schedule for this afternoon so I'll come pick you up at four, all right?"

Four seems an awfully long way off. I feel like I'm being sent to prison. I head for the office. I can feel the eyeballs following me down the hall. New kid, new kid. The grapevine is probably already humming. I know the drill, it's not like I haven't started in a new school in a new place a million times before. That's what happens when your parents hardly ever stay home. Go with the flow. But I'm telling you, I just don't know if I want to be bothered making the effort this time. So do I smile nice and make friends, or dig my heels in and cause a few interesting problems? It's something to think about. And where the heck is the office?

First class is math and there's a test. Everybody's hyper

about it so they barely notice me. I'm excused to look at the text so I can see what they have been studying, so math goes smoothly. Next is English. Book reports. Presentation after presentation. I haven't had to say a word. So far, so good. Then comes geography.

For obvious reasons this is my best subject and I start feeling relaxed. Bad mistake. The geography teacher is different: young, casual, sits on his desk, kids call him by his first name – Ned. He brings the class to order and his eyes immediately go to me.

"Finn, is it?"

"Yes, sir."

The whole class laughs. "You don't need to 'sir' me," says Ned. "I'm just Ned."

"Okay, Ned."

"Welcome to Easthaven, Finn. Why don't you tell us a little bit about yourself so that we can get to know you?"

Why do teachers ask this? It's an impossible question to answer. Say too little and everyone assumes you're hiding something. Say too much and you're either bragging, or boring. There's no way to guess how to hit it just right when you're talking to strangers.

"I'm from Vancouver. I'm staying with my grandmother for the rest of this school year while my parents do some research in Russia." That feels safe enough.

"That's fascinating, Finn," Ned says enthusiastically. "What are your parents' fields of research?"

Uh-oh. This could go either way. "My dad is an anthropologist and my mom is a potamologist."

I can hear the snickers. This is definitely going to go the wrong way.

"So, she what, studies potties? Or, how people go to the potty?" This from the biggest boy in the back of the room. I saw him on my way to the office this morning, shoving some poor kid into a locker.

"Very clever, as always, Fred," Ned says dryly. "Who, besides Finn, knows what a potamologist studies?"

Apparently no one. Big surprise. I'm called upon to explain. It's not the position I want to be in when there is a Fred in the room. Ned wants more. Where in Russia? For how long? Do you ever travel with them? What's that like? The interrogation feels endless and nobody's listening anyway. The minute I add *Dudinka* to *potamologist*, the entire class goes over the edge. They're practically rolling in the aisles, but Ned doesn't seem to notice.

"It all sounds exciting, Finn. I'll bet you wish you were with them."

No kidding.

Lunch could be tricky. Fred's going to have a field day with his potty jokes and, darn it, my invisibility cloak just isn't working today. That bus to Vancouver is looking very good. I pick an empty table at the far side of the cafeteria. It will limit the number of people who witness my humiliation. Or Fred's if I decide to get smart with him, although that's probably not a good idea. He's way bigger than me. The bigger the bully, the smaller the brain, I try to keep remembering that. Right on cue, Fred and his buddies are on my tail with silly grins splitting their faces.

"So, new kid, how do you get to be a potty expert? Do you have to study the dirty magazines in the outhouse?"

Like I haven't heard that before. Fred and his posse surround the table. I think I know how this is going to turn out, except I'm wrong. This girl pushes through the posse and sits down, right across from me.

"Fred! Trying to eat here. Give it a rest." That's all she says but unbelievably, Fred and his boys yuk their way to another table. *That's it?*

"How did you do that?" I ask. "He looks like he eats kids for breakfast."

"He does, but I have special powers," says the girl. "Anyway, this is my table."

"Want me to move?"

"Why? There's an extra chair. Do you stink or something?"

"I don't think so. But I'm the new kid. If I don't work out, your reputation's in the toilet – since we're going for bathroom humour here."

"Hmm," says the girl, looking directly at me for the first time. "I'll take my chances."

A few other kids sit down at the table and start talking to the girl. I settle back in. If this was a book about the tragic story of my exile she'd be beautiful and become my sidekick. There'd be a quest and I'd probably save her. (Okay, I know she was the one who just saved me, but in my story I'd have special powers too. Whatever they are.) She's not bad looking, actually pretty okay, but since she's already lost interest in me the sidekick thing is not looking likely. I open the lunch Gran packed. Finish it. The others talk their way through their lunches, although not to me, and get up to go.

"See you tomorrow?" asks the girl.

"Sure, I guess."

"Okay."

Now that was weird.

"How was your day?" asks Gran at four.

"Not bad."

Gran looks relieved. When we get home, I smell cookies. More bribes. Armstrong is back on his stool, still looking at me as if I'm fallout, so I decide to stare right back. I wonder how old he actually is. His wrinkles are buried so deep in wrinkles that now I'm thinking he's not so much a garden gnome but one of those dogs with the wrinkly faces. And he's trained to protect the farm from fallout like me. The way he stares, he's probably got laser beams in his eyes. If I move he'll shoot me dead. Unfortunately, I can sort of see my dad under the wrinkles, my dad in about a hundred years. Same crazy hair, same bumpy nose, same miniature body. Armstrong? I think we got the wrong name. We should be the Wiry family, or maybe the Gnome family because that's more what we're like. Unfortunately, not a look girls go for. They prefer the Freds of the world. Go figure.

"I'm going to the barn," Armstrong snarls.

Good. The staring contest is over. *What's in that barn?* I wonder. *Does he have animals to look after? He looks kind of old for that.* As he puts his jacket on in the mudroom he fingers my Gore-Tex.

"This your jacket?" he asks. I nod. "You're going to freeze. Your dad must have forgotten that we actually get winter here."

Gran jumps in. "I thought that tomorrow I'd take Finn into Winnipeg after school. We can get him some boots and a warmer jacket. I'll leave your dinner in the oven and Finn and I will eat in town. Is that all right with you?"

Armstrong nods. He's just about to leave when he turns around and glares at me one more time. "The barn is off limits. It's my place, not yours. Understood?"

"No problem."

Except now I really want to know what's in that barn.

CHAPTER 3

Down By the River

The girl's name is Clara. Dark hair, green eyes, athletic looking. Doc Martens and a kilt. Double piercings but no nose ring, which is good because they're gross. The rest of her friends, going clockwise around the table, are Roy, Aaron, Hazel and Jane. This is our fourth lunch together. I'm still thinking about that bus to Vancouver, so I'm not going for friend status or anything, but they're okay from a distance. Roy and Jane are shallow water people. Hazel I'm not sure about and Aaron is pretty sarcastic, so he's hard to figure. Clara is definitely a deep water person. That's the way Dad describes the people he studies, imagery probably compliments of Mom. One type is no better than the other; it's just that shallow water people are the what-you-see-is-what-you-get kind of people, and deep water people are, well, deep. They have secrets, like Armstrong. If I were going for friend status, Clara would be okay. More than okay.

"So are you coming?"

"What?"

Clara's eyebrows are raised. "Were you even listening? Trying to be nice here."

"Sorry. Coming where?"

"To the Forks, this Saturday afternoon. The river's frozen and the Forks has skating trails and a bunch of other stuff. It's supposed to be sunny on the weekend. You do know how to skate, don't you?"

Duh. "How do we get there?"

Clara looks over at Aaron. "Can your mom drive?"

Aaron's in a wheelchair, so he probably doesn't fit into just anybody's car. "Sure. Maybe we can go to a movie after. Let's meet at the school parking lot on Saturday at noon and go from there. I'm sure my mom can drop everybody back home after the movie."

"I'm in. Thanks."

It beats spending Saturday with old people.

Over dinner, I ask about the Forks. No surprise that Gran is all over it. She's pleased I'm making friends, blah, blah, blah. I don't tell her that I'm a long way from making any friends; I just don't want to spend Saturday with her and Armstrong. I mean, I'm angry, but I'm not cruel. After dinner Armstrong disappears to the barn and I help Gran with the dishes then go upstairs to do my homework. But I can't stop thinking about Armstrong. Why does he think he failed with Dad? He helped raise Dad after his own son died, and Dad turned out great. He's smart, respected and has a totally brilliant family if I do say so myself. Armstrong should be proud of his grandson. Does it have something to do with Dad or something to do with Armstrong? And what's in that barn? I really want to know.

I'm tempted to break into the barn, but that approach lacks finesse. I'll use my wiles to break into Armstrong's mind first. Gotta love those wiles. After all, unless I get desperate and take that bus to Vancouver, I've got nothing but time.

On Friday morning in geography, Ned tells us that we are to come to Monday's class wearing all our clothes backwards. Can you believe it? At least I'm not the only one who thinks this is lame; Fred and his posse groan and complain and for once I'm on their side. Ned says it will be an instructive experience.

After school I see Armstrong go into the barn as I'm walking up the lane. What does he do in there? Gran has left a note. She's at her bridge club so there are two plates of dinner in the fridge. Microwave instructions are on a sticky note. Maybe I should just mosey on over to the barn and ask Armstrong when he wants to eat. Maybe I should accidently forget to knock on my way in.

Unfortunately, Armstrong sees me coming. For an old man, he's pretty sharp. He's totally blocking the doorway so I can't see in, but I sure don't smell animals. The only clue to what he was doing is the rag in his hands. It's oily.

"Greasing some machinery, Armstrong? Can I help?"

"No."

No to which question, I wonder. I ask about dinner and he makes it pretty clear he's going to eat alone. I guess I'm still fallout. That leaves me pretty much free so I decide to explore.

The farmhouse is really old, but a real estate agent would say that it's got character. It sits on a bit of a rise and has a great front porch that looks down toward the river. The barn and a couple of equipment sheds are down in that direction. Behind the house there's an apple orchard and some fields. There's a road there too, running parallel to the river. You can take that road straight into Winnipeg or turn right to cross the river and get to Easthaven. I decide to check out the equipment sheds near the river, but there's hardly anything in them. No animals, no equipment. So if Armstrong got rid of all his farm equipment and all his animals, what's left in the barn? What needs oiling and why won't he show me?

Beyond the sheds is the Red River. Mom has studied it, of course; everybody has. It's not as exciting as the Yenisei or even the Nile. It could be exciting because every year it floods, but it's not, because everybody knows where and when the flood is coming. It's about as exciting as reading a murder mystery when you already know who the murderer is and when he's going to strike.

The river, completely frozen and covered with snow, sure doesn't look very exciting right now. I wonder if you could actually skate all the way to the Forks? Probably. But you'd have to shovel a path through the snow for something like forty kilometres. No, going with Clara to a place where somebody else shovels all the snow off the river is a better plan. Come to think of it, going any place with Clara is a better plan.

Our farm is on the west side of the river, at the edge of the village. Just down the road is the Ste. Agathe church. Surrounded by snow, it looks almost like a cathedral and I can imagine that I'm somewhere in Europe. I wish.

The hairs on my arms prickle. I thought I was alone, but I swear I see a shadow on the riverbank. A bear? No. Gotta stop thinking about Vancouver. An antelope?

I look down the bank. Not four metres away from me is this guy, almost hidden from sight underneath a clump of trees by the edge of the ice. He's not young, maybe thirty. And he's dressed up as if he's pretending to be an old-time trapper or something, in wool pants, leather lace-up boots and a thick, red plaid jacket. The whole scene is a little off-kilter. Like someone took a photograph, ripped it down the middle then taped it back together crooked. My gut tells me I should back away and I've been taught to listen to that little voice. But who is he? What's he doing on the property? Should I call Armstrong? That idea is enough to make me stay put. It's not as if the guy is threatening. Maybe he's homeless or something.

"Hey," I call out.

The guy looks up at me. "Oh, hello. Are you new around here?"

"Yeah. Visiting my grandmother."

"And who might she be?"

Was he for real? "Mrs. Armstrong. This is her property, actually."

"Ah, the lovely Caroline. Such a help to Armstrong."

"You know my great-grandfather?"

"I do."

"Who are you? What are you doing here?" For some reason I'm feeling invaded, even though it's not exactly my farm.

The guy smiles and leans back into the bank. "Enjoying the river. This is one of my favourite spots. Armstrong never minds if I come and visit it, especially in springtime."

I snort. "There's not much to enjoy. You did notice that

the river is frozen? And that it's only February? It's hardly springtime."

The man laughs. "In the ice it's springtime. It's deciding how long the river needs its blanket, how much longer it can rest. Because when it wakes, it has work to do. How much work depends on the kind of sleep it's had."

I get it. I'm not my mother's son for nothing. "You mean how much flooding it will do depends on the climate conditions of the past winter."

"Very clever! That's exactly it. And I love listening to the ice think about it."

"You mean, listening to the cracks and pressure shifts and pretending it's talking to you?" Maybe the guy's a poet.

"Nothing so mundane. I listen to the flow of water underneath the ice. Rivers always flow, even when they're sleeping. It's their job. They flow and flow until they meet an obstacle and even then they don't stop. A river always finds a way to keep flowing, no matter what the obstacle might be."

Definitely a poet; an out-of-work, homeless poet. Why else would he spout touchy-feelie stuff like this? "Who are you? How do you know Armstrong and Gran?"

"Armstrong and I have been friends for a long time. I told you I loved this spot, and Armstrong does too. In the summer, we fish and talk about the river. He loves it as much as I do, you know."

Huh. He can't have known Armstrong for too long because he's nowhere near old enough. But Dad always said that deep water people have old souls so maybe that's the connection. Anybody who talks like this guy has got to be deep water, no question. But he hardly seems the type to be friends with Armstrong. Although how would I know? I'm surprised that Armstrong even *has* a friend.

The guy stands up. "Would you like to fish with me?"

"You mean, next summer?"

"No, tomorrow morning. I'm going ice fishing early in the morning. I'll show you how."

"Uh…maybe. I might want to sleep in." *Why's he asking me? Why not Armstrong? Maybe now's when I should be backing away.*

"I'll be here early, whether you come or not. Have a good evening." With that, the guy walks away, heading down the frozen riverbank toward the bridge.

"Hey! What's your name?" I shout after him. But he just keeps going.

Several times that evening, I open my mouth to ask Armstrong about the guy by the river but each time I close it again. I feel stupid that I didn't even get the guy's name. Maybe I will go ice fishing with him. He's strange but I don't think he's *bad* strange. It's not as if I've got anything else to do until it's time to go to the Forks. Besides, I've never been ice fishing before. Might as well make good use of my brand new winter coat.

I roll over in bed and squint at the clock on the night table. It's 6:55. My room is dark and the house is still. For a minute I think about going back to sleep, but that turns out to be impossible. I'm curious about ice fishing. Actually, I'm more curious about the guy than I am about the fishing. There's something odd about him and I want to figure out what.

Before I have second thoughts, I get up and dressed. Quietly I head to the front door and pull on my new winter gear. Making sure not to let the door bang shut, I start off toward the river and the hint of dawn just beyond it. Over the crunch of my boots in the snow I hear him before I see him.

"Good morning. Glad you decided to join me. Come take a look if you like."

At the edge of the ice I peer through the darkness and see the guy standing practically, but not quite, in the middle of the river. It must be safe because the ice isn't cracking around him. I guess it's okay. Carefully, I walk across the river, leaving a trail of footsteps on the fresh expanse of snow. He's standing by a perfectly round hole in the ice holding a tree branch with a string tied on the end. That's how you ice fish? It looks pretty low tech. Then again, if he's homeless he probably can't afford anything else.

"Don't you need a proper rod and reel and lures and stuff? And I thought ice fishermen had little huts and stoves to keep them warm."

"Some do, but it feels like cheating to me. I prefer an honest fight between man and beast. Ice fishing is about the rhythm of the river. In summer, the fish behave one way and in winter, another. To challenge the truly mighty channel cats you must learn their rhythms. Armstrong knows this. Ask him. He knows the secrets that a great river like the Red holds in its deeps. Your mother does too, she should have taught you that."

Channel cats? Rhythms? Armstrong knows the secret of the deeps? *And just how does this guy know my mother?*

That photograph I was talking about? It just slipped another centimetre off-centre. "Who *are* you?"

But the guy doesn't answer because there's a tug on his line. Wrong word, actually. The whole branch gets jerked out of his hand and would have gone right down the hole except it catches crosswise.

"Help me!"

There's something about hearing the word *help* that inspires action, whether you want to help or not. I run the last few steps. He picks up the branch and pulls and I start bringing in the line hand over hand. No fancy rod and reel for this guy, that's for sure. There's gotta be a whale on the other end. Has to be, because it weighs a tonne. There's pressure as I pull on the string and I know whatever is hooked is coming closer to the surface. All of a sudden it decides to put up a fight. I can't see the thrashing, but I sure can feel it. The string hurts, even though I'm wearing gloves, and I let go with a shout, I can't help it. The guy keeps pulling and pulling until there's a snap. Whatever it was is gone.

We're both breathing kind of heavy.

"Sorry about the line," I say. "What was that?"

"Finn, I would like to introduce you to Charlie. It would have been nice for you to meet face to face, but Charlie is particularly touchy in the winter. Don't worry, there will be other meetings."

"Charlie?"

"Charlie is a channel cat, a catfish. The Red River is known for its catfish. They are very strong and love a fight. Very much like your great-grandfather. That's why he gets along with them so well."

"How do you know that one was Charlie? Do you name all

the fish?" This guy is a nutbar.

"I know all my cats," the guy says smugly. "Charlie is the biggest, the oldest and the wisest."

You know when little old ladies describe themselves as cat people? Well, this guy gives new meaning to the term. I don't know a lot about fish. That's a different kind of -ologist, and I don't hang with them much. But I'm pretty sure that catfish aren't at the top of most fishermen's lists. Trash fish, bottom feeders, ugly as sin: that's what I think of when I think of catfish. I know some people think they're good eating, but I don't think I could forget what the catfish ate before I ate the catfish. And secrets? That would be like hiding a secret in a dumpster. On the other hand, I kind of like the idea of big fish patrolling up and down the river, fish so smart they can escape from the fishermen. The more they escape, the wiser they become, so over time they become one with the river, secret-keepers for the great river god. But if I was the river god and wanted one of my creatures to keep my secrets I'd pick a better fish, like a trout or a bass. On second thought, keeping your secret in an ugly bottom-feeder would be safer.

Okay, getting carried away here. This guy is contagious.

"I don't get it. If the fish is your...friend, why do you want to catch it?"

The nutbar throws the wrecked fishing pole down into the hole and walks to the bank. He sits on a snowbank and stretches his legs out. I don't. Why soak my butt?

"Friends? No. We are foes, but we respect one another. The tug of war between fish and fisherman involves strategy, strength, cunning and patience. Fishing is a form of communication, just like talking is for us. We take turns leading the conversation, but we both learn from the discussion. And what we learn helps each of us to survive."

As the sky grows brighter, the conversation gets weirder. I mean, come on. I shiver, even though I'm not really all that cold. I guess the nutbar notices.

"It's getting light. Armstrong will be up soon," he says. "You should probably go or he'll wonder where you are. I will see you again, Finn."

I look up at the sky and see that he's right, although Armstrong couldn't care less where I am. I look back and the guy is already walking away. He's not much for goodbyes. I climb back up the bank to the farmhouse.

Dad says when you meet a stranger both your brain and your gut get involved. Your brain lets you learn one or two facts about him, your gut tells you whether he's a good guy or a bad guy, and between the two you decide to see him again, or not. Some people like lots of facts before they let their gut kick in. People like my dad go gut-first, and his gut makes him really good at making the other person feel comfortable. Comfort makes the person want to talk to him and, in the end, he gets lots and lots of facts. It's what makes Dad a good scientist, that combo of gut and brain.

Right now I have a lot of gut and very little brain. My gut says that there's something off about this guy and I should stay away. But my brain says not to go so fast. The way he talks and the clothes he wears are really old-fashioned, but that could be because of where he comes from, or maybe they're hand-me-downs. Not a big deal. He's a fisherman, so that whole communication thing probably wasn't creepy, just weird fish lore. Okay, he didn't give me his name. But Charlie interrupted, so it's not like he was avoiding the question. We just got distracted. The main problem is this: he knows way more than he should about my family. And it's not just that he knows my mother has a thing for rivers. Did you notice? He knows my name and I'm certain I never told him.

The only explanation for that is that this guy and Armstrong are talking about me behind my back. Yeah, they probably hang out in the barn. No wonder I'm not allowed in.

And that really burns me.

CHAPTER 4

The Forks

When I get back to the farmhouse, Gran is up and cooking to beat the band. She believes in a hearty breakfast. Three eggs, toast, fried potatoes, tomato slices and a side of fruit and yogurt are a little more than I'm used to facing. But there it is, all on my plate the minute I arrive in the kitchen, so I pick up my fork and dig in anyway. Gran is pleased that I've taken an interest in exploring. I don't actually lie, but I neglect to tell her I wasn't exactly alone. And there's no sign of Armstrong, so he clearly didn't even notice that I was gone.

"Eat up. You'll need the energy," Gran says. "It'll be cold out on the river. There are warming huts here and there at the Forks so make sure you use them."

By eleven-thirty we're in the car and on our way to Easthaven. Aaron's mom is going to meet us in the high school parking lot. I have my new coat and boots and a backpack full of borrowed socks, mitts and scarves – enough so that I wonder if maybe we're actually going to the North Pole. The transfer is successful. Gran drives away with a wave and we're off. Roy is riding shotgun. Hazel, Jane and Clara are squeezed in the back leaving the middle for Aaron's wheelchair and me. Roy can't stop talking about the Manitoba Moose. At first, I think he means the animals, but it turns out that it's the local hockey team. My bad but hey, I'm a Canucks fan.

"So Carlyle is taking over for Perron as head coach, but Perron says he's going to take the team to court! Nobody cares because the Moose are finally winning. There's a game tonight, but my dad sold our season's tickets when the team was losing so badly so I can't go. Bummer, eh? Do you play?"

I'm trying to catch up and replay the conversation in my head. Finally I get to the actual question.

"Nope. I mean, look at me. Way better to leave team sports to the big guys. I don't like getting crushed on a regular basis."

"I hear ya," says Roy with a sigh. "I'm on the Grunthal Bantam "B" Team. We're not having our best year."

Aaron looks at me kind of close. "You could be a jockey," he says. "Or the guy who gets shot out of a cannon."

"Gee, thanks," I say. I check my backpack. "Sorry, I left my cannon in my other pack." If he thinks he's going to get to me he's going to have to think again. My size has been mocked by the best.

"Too bad," he comes back. "It would be fun to watch."

"Ewww! That's gross," says Clara.

"Well I dunno," says Aaron dryly. "It would be less violent than hockey." Everybody laughs and Roy's fist comes from the front seat and punches Aaron's shoulder.

"Gimme a break. We can't all ride around on a throne! Somebody's got to let himself get beat up for your entertainment. Let's have some respect!"

After that, I guess I can stop ignoring the wheelchair. "What happened to your legs?"

"I got run over by a bale of hay."

"What?"

"I'm not kidding. It rolled off the baler by accident, ran over my legs and just kept on going. After me, it knocked down an electrical pole and crushed a truck before it stopped. Talk about momentum, because it wasn't like it was rolling down a hill or anything. I remember lying there in the field watching it go, thinking the bale was like that runaway gingerbread man in the story, do you remember? 'You can't catch me, I'm the hay bale man!'"

"That's just so random!"

"Yeah, that's me, random," sighs Aaron. Then he leans over and whispers, "but it's great for the sympathy vote. Girls love the chair."

Hazel groans, "Yeah, right." Everybody laughs and Aaron grins at me.

I grin back. He's okay. "So what do you guys do for fun around here, besides hockey and skating and shooting short guys from cannons? No downhill skiing, obviously." Roy snickers.

Clara leans over the seat. "Some people ski cross-country on the river trails. It's just as much fun as skating."

"What about…ice fishing? Is that popular?"

There's sudden interest coming from the wheelchair. It's like this wall of energy coming at me.

"Ice fishing is great. Me and my dad share a hut with some guys from his work. The riverbanks here aren't too steep, which works for my chair, and once I'm on the ice I'm good."

Jane shivers. "The ice fishermen have these little huts with heaters in them that they put over top of the holes they drill, but I still think I'd freeze to death. And it's gotta be so boring!"

"Are you interested in ice fishing, Finn?" asks Aaron's mom in a worried voice. "It's quite dangerous, especially on the river."

"Why especially on the river, Mrs. Taylor?"

"Because under the ice the water is running, it's not still water like a lake. Running water doesn't freeze as well or as evenly. If you don't know the currents, you might get onto thin ice and fall through."

Well, that wouldn't be good. I grin. "So, this skating today, it's all just a ploy to lure the new guy onto thin ice and get rid of him, eh?"

Roy pretends to hit me. He seems to like hitting. Mrs. Taylor is spluttering about all the research that the city does to test the ice, that's why everybody has to wait until it's safe, etc., etc.

As we drive into the parking lot at the Forks, it's like a festival. I see kids with snowboards, hockey players, moms and dads with little kids, horse-drawn wagons, stores and toboggans, and that's before I'm even out of the car. Very cool. We all hop out and Mrs. Taylor leaves to go do her shopping or whatever. Clara leads the way toward some shops, and I'm a little worried until I see a sign that says SKATE RENTALS. Hazel and I have to rent. We get that sorted then head toward the trail. But I'm busy looking behind me, because that's where the snowboarders are heading. They've actually built a snow park beside the river for the boarders. Now this has possibilities because boarding is something I'm good at. I'm from Vancouver, remember? But for now, we're skating.

We lace up at one of the warming huts. Hazel begins to

recite facts for the tourist. That would be me. "It's called the Forks because it's where the Assiniboine and the Red rivers meet. It's been a meeting place for thousands of years. In winter, after the ice freezes and the city clears the snow, it's the longest naturally frozen skating trail in the world."

I interrupt. "Isn't that the Rideau Canal in Ottawa?"

Hazel glares at me. "No way. Theirs is wider but ours is longer. It's even in the *Guinness Book of World Records*, so that proves it."

"Okay, okay!"

We all push off onto the ice. Roy's got his hockey stick just in case he runs into an impromptu game. I push Aaron's chair. The girls are talking about shoes or something. There are little kids in helmets pushing ice walkers, teenagers hanging out in the warming huts, dads pulling toboggans, even a row of ice fishermen along the bank. I look at Aaron and he nods, so I push over that way.

"What are you fishing for?" Aaron asks.

One of the guys looks up. "Walleye, mostly."

"Anything that bites," says another guy, and they all laugh.

I'm curious. "Do you ever catch channel cats?"

"Yeah, some," replies the first guy. "I usually throw them back."

"Why?"

"Well, they're better for catching than eating. There are other fish that make better eating. Catching them though, that can get pretty interesting. There are some pretty big cats down there and they can fight like nobody's business. I had one last year that really made me sweat. I like to throw 'em back. Then they get bigger and stronger and there'll be another fight in my future. Round and round it goes, kid."

"Are they hard to catch in the winter?"

It's Aaron who answers this one. "Hard to find, more like. I think they go deep."

But the nutbar found Charlie. "So, keeper of the river's secrets, would ya say?"

The fishermen look at me strangely. "You could say that, I suppose. Who are you, anyway?"

"Finn Armstrong. I'm visiting my grandmother for a while."

"Armstrong? You related to that old fella down in Ste. Agathe?"

"He's my great-grandfather."

"Well, no wonder you're askin' about channel cats then." The men all laugh. "See ya, kid."

So what was that supposed to mean?

"How'd you hear about channel cats?" asks Aaron.

"Just a guy I met by the river. He was going on about 'the tug of war between fish and fisherman' being some kind of conversation about survival or something. I'm no fisherman so it mostly went over my head. But I liked the way he talked about the channel cats. He even names them!"

"That's not so weird," replies Aaron seriously. "Lots of fishermen get attached to the big cats. I like fishing for them because I like a good fight, just don't ask me to eat one. Ugh."

"You said it," I laugh. "That's exactly what I thought when he started talking about catfish as if they were river gods or something. He was really out there."

"Who was he? Maybe I know him," asks Aaron.

"Dunno. He didn't tell me his name," I reply. "What do you think that fisherman meant about my great-grandfather?"

"No idea," replies Aaron.

We push back over to the girls. "Where'd you go?" Clara asks. She looks good on skates.

"Just talking to those fishermen."

We skate back to the warming hut. I unlace and Jane says, "What's your hurry? Aren't you going to keep skating? We're not getting picked up for another hour."

"I'm going snowboarding. Want to come?"

I'm no star, but I'm not bad. And the competition is probably going to be less fierce in Winnipeg than on Grouse Mountain. Showing off? Yeah, absolutely. You can rent boards at the skate shop so I get myself set up and head for the snowboard park. It's got rails, tabletops and a few jumps. Nothing big, but Clara's watching, so I pull out all the stops and hope I don't have any spectacular falls. I don't.

Later, we eat at the food fair then go see a movie. The girls want *Titanic*, the guys want *Men in Black*, so we compromise on *The Lost World: Jurassic Park*. The movie makes me think of the nutbar — I keep imagining channel cats as killer dinosaur fish. I mean, they've got the faces for it. In the car, I say that to Aaron and he snorts. Then Roy starts humming the theme from *Jaws* and I start talking about a zombie catfish apocalypse and we're laughing so hard that Clara drops her popcorn bag and we both dive for it before it spills all over the car and our hands touch because we both grab the bag at the same time. And after that I stop thinking about the zombie catfish apocalypse and just think about Clara's hand.

Gran is waiting, and the kitchen light is still on when Mrs. Taylor drives up the lane. Maybe not going to Russia with my parents isn't such a bad thing after all. Gran thanks Mrs. Taylor, and then she thanks Clara for showing me around. Clara looks a little embarrassed and that's when I get it. I am such an idiot. Clara didn't sit at my table in the cafeteria by accident, she was told to be nice to me. What did Gran do, bribe her with cookies? I'm so mad I can barely say goodbye. After they go, Gran asks me if I want to go straight to bed or have a hot chocolate first.

"Hot chocolate?! No! I can't believe you told Clara to be nice to me! I don't need a babysitter!" I'm grinding my teeth I'm so mad.

"But Finn! Clara's mother and I are in the same bridge club. It was nothing, really. Clara said she was happy to do it. And knowing somebody always makes it easier to make friends." Gran truly doesn't see the problem.

"I don't want to make friends. Get it? I'm not staying here!"

Next morning, I wait until Gran leaves for church and Armstrong is locked up in his mysterious barn. What do I care what's in there? He could be building a spaceship for all I care. I pack my duffel bag. I reckon if I walk to Highway 75 I can hitch a ride to Winnipeg and then a bus to Vancouver. I've got friends I can stay with in Vancouver. *Real* friends.

It's a great idea, but there's one small problem. Nobody picks me up. All I'm getting are glares from drivers. Even the transport drivers just give me a look and keep going. I thought they were supposed to like having company. Can't anybody give me a break? Finally a black pickup stops. The driver rolls down the passenger window, but he doesn't open the door.

"Do you need help, kid? Is there somebody I can call for you?" he calls out.

"I just need a ride to the Forks," I shout through the window.

The driver looks me up and down suspiciously. "Your parents know you're hitching?"

I hesitate a second too long.

"Look, kid. I'm happy to call child services or something if you need to get out. I'll wait right here until they come. But I can't put you in my car. You understand, don't you?"

Inside I groan. That is so not the issue here. I just want a ride! The driver's sitting there, waiting. I hate it that grown-ups hold all the cards. When do I get to be in charge?

I wave the guy off. The next five cars pass without stopping. What the heck? Am I wearing a sign that says "RUNAWAY"?

Finally, there's nothing to do but go back. Going home isn't happening. I trudge back and dump my duffel inside the front door. Gran's going to be ages; she helps at the church luncheon and doesn't get home until dinnertime. Armstrong, well, whatever. I can't stand to be inside so I head down to the river.

I don't see the nutbar. There was a wind last night that blew most of the snow off river, leaving a clean sheet of ice. It's just as nice as the groomed ice trail at the Forks so I step out. Who needs skates? I take a running leap and slide toward the other side of the river. It's not snowboarding, but it's not bad either. Back again. And again. A little farther each time as I find the right stance.

Hate this place.

Slide.

Hate this place.
Slide.
Hate this place.
Slide.
"Stop!"

I dig my heels in and whip my head toward the voice just as I hear the first crack. I watch as cracks start to spread out from underneath my heels. Everything's in slow motion. One crack catches my eye and I follow it. Then another. My eyes follow it as it radiates outward, moving closer and closer to the bank. I'm standing in the middle of a star. I stop breathing.

"Slowly, slowly, Finn. Bend your knees, get low. That's right. Put your hands down on the ice very gently. Now try to transfer your weight so you've got half on your hands and half on your feet. Right. Go slow. You have to get into a starfish position, belly on the ice. You need to spread your weight over as much surface as you can. Slide out very slowly. Every shift has got to be gentle or you'll go through."

Still not breathing over here. My thighs are killing me in the squat, but I'm afraid to put my knees down. They'll go through, I know they will. I can hear rushing water below me; my slide must have taken me right over the main current. I spread my knees, froggie style, and then slide forward so my inner thighs, not my knees, touch first. The tension is making my muscles shake so much I'm sure the vibration alone is going to break the ice. When I finally get my belly down, I start breathing again. I can feel the current flowing beneath me. I close my eyes, but visions of zombie catfish show up underneath my eyelids and they're not funny any more.

"You're doing great. Now you want to use your fingers and your toes to push forward, an inch at a time. Try to use all four limbs at once to keep your body weight distributed."

I try. The ice is too slippery.

"I can't."

"Take your gloves off, Finn. The nylon isn't helping."

I wiggle out of the gloves and dig my nails in. The cold under my nails makes my back teeth hurt. How can that be?

"Finn, don't stop! Your body heat will melt the top layer of ice and you'll stick. You have to keep going!"

Okay. Keep going. One inch at a time. *How did I get so far from shore?* My fingers are numb but sweat is pouring off my forehead. Another inch. Another. My nose is cold, hovering a hair's breadth over the ice. It's dripping snot. Gross. More cracking all around me. *Concentrate.*

And then the nutbar grabs my wrist and hauls me off the ice.

"Breathe," he says. "You did great."

It's a few minutes before that whole breathing thing comes back properly, but finally I can do it without thinking about it.

"What's your name, anyway?" I ask, still feeling a bit wobbly.

"Peter. Peter de Meuron."

"Well, thank you, Peter de Meuron. I mean it. You saved me, man."

"Glad I was here," he says. "What were you doing way out there?"

I think about this, then look sideways at Peter. He just saved my life, so I guess he deserves the truth. It's not as though anybody else around here is willing to listen to me.

"Running away."

Now it's Peter's turn to be quiet.

"And did it work?"

I snort. "Almost permanently."

Peter looks at me in shock. Then his mouth starts to twitch, and in a second we're both laughing.

CHAPTER 5

Those Who Stay

Monday morning when I get off the school bus, Clara's waiting for me in the parking lot. I ignore her, but she's not so easy to shake off.

"Stop it!" she says, and she grabs my arm. "So my mom and your grandmother asked me to sit with you at lunch. Big deal. Turns out you weren't a complete dork, at least I didn't think so until now. I didn't have to invite you to the Forks, you know, but I wanted you to come. So can you get over yourself?"

"You can drop the friend routine now. I'm fine on my own."

"Good for you. Moving on. What are you wearing backwards for geography? Some people are really getting into it. The get-ups are insane." She doesn't stop talking as we walk into the school, so I guess that's what she means when she says "moving on." I have more to say but she doesn't give me a chance. And then it's too late because geography is starting.

I decide that the only thing I'm going to wear backwards is my T-shirt. It's the least ridiculous and the easiest to turn right way around as soon as geography is over. Everybody's pretty hyper going in to class, as if acting like we're still in kindergarten is some kind of big deal. This thing is so lame. This whole school is lame.

Ned gets everybody quiet then he looks around. Jane's wearing a blouse that's supposed to button up the front only today, the buttons run down the back. Aaron is wearing his boots on the wrong feet. And Fred's wearing a Toronto Maple Leafs jersey back to front, but as big as Fred is, the jersey is even bigger. It must be his dad's shirt or something. I'm telling you, I've been to a lot of schools in my time and this level of audience participation, when even the bullies get into it, is more than a little weird.

"Okay, class, so how do your clothes feel?"

I close my eyes. Save me from overenthusiastic teachers, *pleeeease*. But incredibly, the class is with him.

"They don't fit."

"I needed help with the buttons."

"I had to get a bigger size." This from Fred. Class participation or bragging? I'm voting for bragging.

"I feel twisted, as if my clothes are going the wrong way."

"Precisely! *Your clothes are going the wrong way.* Well done, class. Now what does all of this have to do with geography?"

Nothing, as far as I can tell. Ned keeps talking. "We all live on the banks of the Red River. Tell me, what direction does it run?"

Well, duh. It runs down. All rivers do. But apparently that's not the answer. Hazel has her hand up first. "It runs from south to north."

"Correct. It runs backwards."

Sorry, Ned, but that's not right. I have to jump in. "Lots of rivers run south to north. It's not backwards. A river runs down from its headwaters to its mouth, and that can be in any direction."

"Ah, now we see the value of potamology. Finn, you are absolutely right." I cringe. Why did I open my mouth? "But if a river runs down, that means the headwaters of a river are higher than the mouth, correct?"

We all nod.

"So compare the temperature of the headwaters to the water at the mouth. Which is likely to be colder?"

I think about this. It would make sense that most of the time the headwaters would be in the mountains and probably colder than the mouth. "The headwaters," I say.

"Is this the case with our Red River?"

Okay, he's got me going. "No, it isn't. The headwaters start way down south, so they're warmer than the mouth." Now I get it: in terms of temperature the Red River runs from warm to cold. It runs backwards.

"Now we're getting to the exciting part." Ned rubs his hands together. Mom would like him, he's really getting into it. "So what's the problem with running backwards?"

Now I'm really confused. All of us are. Why is it a problem?

I close my eyes, because it's easier to think. The river will thaw first in the United States because that's south, and that's where it will warm up first. The meltwater will run north, because that's the direction the river flows. But farther north, the river is still frozen. So the meltwater is going to run into an ice jam. And then, then…the river is going to flood.

I get it. One by one, everybody in the class has their own little eureka moment. We know the river floods regularly, and now we know why.

Ned, this is very cool stuff.

There's a buzz as we leave the classroom. On the school bus home I start composing an email to Mom in my head. She's going to love the way Ned described everything. I'm still full of it as I walk up the lane to the house. It's chocolate cake today, and I cut myself a huge piece. Armstrong glares at me, but he's already chowing down on a piece that's just as big so I ignore him.

"How was school?" asks Gran.

"Totally awesome," I say with my mouth full. She looks surprised. No wonder. She's been the only cheerful person in this house since I got here.

"No really, I mean it," I say. I tell her all about Ned's class. And strangely, Armstrong looks interested.

"About time they started teaching something worth learning at that school," he grumbles.

Gran starts telling me about some of the floods she's been through then she says, "Tell Finn about the flood of 1950, Armstrong."

"Yeah, Armstrong, what happened?" I suppose I can make an effort too. Moving on, and all that. Armstrong shoots his blue laser eyes my way. Then he actually answers. Amazing.

"We hadn't had a really bad flood for nearly a hundred years. Nobody was ready. Hardly anybody had dikes and the experts didn't really know how to predict how high the water would get. A lot of towns south of here were completely flooded. And in the end, we nearly lost the city, too." Armstrong shook his head.

"I told them, but they wouldn't listen. I knew it was going to be bad."

Gran patted his hand. "Yes, but after that flood, they built the floodway. You helped talk them into it."

"What's the floodway?"

"It's a big ditch, kind of like a moat, along the eastern side of the city," explains Gran. "It's supposed to take the overflow from the Red River and divert it around the city. A lot of people thought we were crazy to build it. But it was supposed to save the city from flooding, and so far, it has."

"You said you knew it was going to be bad. How did you know?" As soon as I ask Armstrong gets up to leave.

"I just knew," he growls. And that's that. Family time is over. Gran sighs then retreats to her fallback position.

"More cake, Finn?"

If Armstrong doesn't lighten up I'm going to weigh a thousand pounds.

"No, thanks. Is he always like this, or is it just me?"

"You being here has brought up a lot of memories, Finn. He's struggling. Give him a chance."

"What kind of memories?"

"Like I said before, it has to do with passing things down."

"What, does he still want my dad to come back and take over the farm or something?"

"No, it's much more complicated than that. Don't worry about it, Finn. He'll eventually come around."

"But what do I say to him? Is there anything I can say that won't make him mad?" Armstrong's really starting to bug me. I don't know why Gran puts up with him.

"Finn, some people are flexible, they seem to flow like the river. Your dad is one of those people and so are you, whether you feel that way right now or not. Other people are strong and solid – some might say rigid. They stay put and fight the flow. Armstrong is one of those. We need both kinds of people, don't you think? Those who go, and those who stay."

I sigh.

"Gran, somebody told me Armstrong was a fisherman. Does he like to fish?"

"Oh, yes," she laughs. "He's famous! He's small but has always been strong so he could fight with the biggest of the channel cats. But he got his reputation more because of the way he could find them. It's like they came to him. There'd be days that the other fishermen couldn't even get a nibble, but Armstrong was never skunked." Gran looked thoughtful. "It's the fight he loves, I think. He's always fought the river. Besting the fish that live in the Red was one way to fight, I guess."

Gran gets up and rinses the plates. "But at his age, it's more thinking than doing. His favourite spot is just down behind the equipment sheds, but he rarely goes any more." She sighs. "Why do you ask?"

I don't want to tell her about Peter. "I saw some ice fishermen at the Forks. When I told them my name they seemed to know Armstrong."

"That's not surprising. He's pretty famous around here."
For fishing?"

Gran frowns. "Not just fishing."

I try and try, but she won't tell me anything else.

CHAPTER 6

Peter

March 1997

Weekends are totally boring in Ste. Agathe. There is no place to go and no one to hang with. I play video games on my laptop for a while, but playing by myself gets old fast. "Stop rattling around," orders Armstrong. "When I was a boy there was always lots to do."

Yeah, thanks Armstrong; that really helps. Just to get out of his way I head outside. It would be cool if he had some animals, a horse or some cows or even pigs. Lots of people around here raise pigs. They're supposed to be really clean animals but boy, do those farms stink. I head toward the barn. Rare enough that Armstrong's not guarding the door, so I walk around to the back where he can't see me and try to find a crack. I almost think I can see something between two boards when I hear Armstrong's voice.

"See anything?" he asks sarcastically.

I bite my lip. Bummer. But what the heck, he's not yelling at me yet. I decide to keep pushing.

"It's kind of a rule that the less you tell me about what's in the barn the more I'm going to want to know. So what are you greasing up in there – an old car? A World War II motorbike? Your rifle collection? Harness for an invisible flying horse?" That almost gets me a smile. Unbelievable. But then the yelling starts and I still don't know anything.

So much for spying. I decide to check out the river and see if Peter's there.

He is.

"Welcome, Finn. Lovely day, isn't it?" Peter's sitting on a snowdrift. Patting the snow beside him, he offers me a seat. Is he kidding? How is it that he's okay with freezing his butt off? "Smell that earth!"

I sniff but all I smell is snow. I think he's getting a little ahead of himself, seasons-wise. We sit quiet for a minute. I know he saved my life and all, but I'm still ticked that he and Armstrong are all over my life story behind my back. What about his story? It's only fair that I know.

"So, have you lived around here for a long time?"

"Oh, yes, a very long time. But I'm originally from Switzerland."

That accounts for the accent. "Why'd you come to Canada?"

Peter smiles. "For adventure, of course! My whole family came because we thought Canada sounded so very exciting. It's wonderful to be able to see new places, don't you think?"

Now that's something I get. "I was supposed to go to Egypt. But then my parents got this really important gig in Russia so they had to go there."

"I'll bet that was disappointing, " says Peter.

"Nah, that kind of stuff just happens when you're a scientist. I'm okay with it," I say. I say that because it makes it sound as if my parents didn't just dump me, but actually now it kind of feels true. Peter says his father was a farmer, but he's dead now.

"Does your family still own a farm around here?"

"No, it's long gone to others. But I come back often because I love it here."

"Was your dad upset when he had to sell?"

"Very upset, but we had no choice. It was the river, you see. There was a terrible flood, the worst ever, and it took everything we had." Peter looks sad just thinking about it.

"It's hard to believe that this river can do stuff like that," I say. "What happened?"

Peter is quiet for a minute. Then he starts. "It was a hard, hard winter. The snow and sleet were endless, drifting higher than the window sills then freezing hard. The temperature was frigid for weeks and the ice in the river must have been five feet thick. We didn't think that spring would ever come but finally it did. Spring always comes, eventually. That year it came all at once, warming up over a very few days. The snow melted and the ice in the river started to crack and break up and we were so relieved that winter was finally over. The thing was, we were new here and didn't understand what all those signs meant.

"One day, around the beginning of May I think, the day was really warm and there was a strong south wind blowing. You could hear the water trickling into the river as the snow melted. And in the space of twenty-four hours, the river rose nine feet. Nine feet! Even those who had lived here for a long time had never seen anything like it. But just up at the Forks there was a big ice jam, you know, where the two rivers meet. The river backed up behind the ice and spilled over its banks. It happened so fast that we could barely save ourselves, much less anything else. Houses got knocked off their footings, children were screaming, it was awful. We had to cut a hole in our roof and climb through it so we wouldn't drown. From up on the roof all you could see was a sea full of people's belongings streaming past and animals desperately swimming for high ground. It was a terrible sight. Something bumped into our house and it knocked me off the roof. I don't remember much after that."

Peter frowns. "We were rescued by a stranger with a boat, but had to leave everything behind. So my family left. It had all been too much."

"Wow." I lean against the bank. "That really must have sucked."

Peter smiles. "You could say that."

"But it all worked out, didn't it? I mean, you were okay and you came back, so it's all good, right?"

Peter goes still. "Not really," he replies quietly.

I can tell from the tone of his voice that I shouldn't ask anything else. The conversation is over.

After Peter leaves, there's no place to go but back to the house. Gran and Armstrong are at the kitchen table. They're playing cribbage, and when I see what they're doing I start to grin. Yeah, yeah, I know, it's a game that's like, from the dark ages, but I am really good at it. My dad taught me and we play all the time. I'm *really* good.

"Wanna play three-handed?" Gran looks surprised, and the

old man focuses his laser eyes on me. Then he starts to smile, real slow. "By all means," he says.

Oh, I'm gonna get him. We play one round of three-handed then Gran escapes 'cause Armstrong and I are in a different league. I don't mean to brag; it's just the truth. Armstrong cuts for deal.

"Fifteen-two and the rest won't do."

"Fifteen-four and the rest don't score."

"Fifteen-two, fifteen-four plus three for the run and I've got the knob."

I win the first game, Armstrong the second. I am absolutely going to take the rubber. It's tough, but I get the cards, and not only do I win the third game, I darn near skunk Armstrong. He's spitting mad and I love it. We go again. And again. Gran's starting to get worried because we won't come for dinner. We're not hungry. We go again.

Finally Armstrong yells uncle. "I'm going to the barn," he says.

"Can I come?" I ask innocently.

"Shut up," he growls and I have to laugh.

Then he spears me with his eyes again and says, "Rematch. Tomorrow."

"You're on."

And then, just when he's heading out of the mudroom and thinks I can't hear him he says under his breath, "At least the kid inherited something from me."

Oh, yeah.

Next morning we're up early. Armstrong's eyes are gleaming. I don't know, maybe he studied some book titled *Greatest*

Cribbage Games of All Time or something last night. Whatever he did, he's on fire this morning. Don't worry, I win enough to hold my head up but just barely. This time, I'm the one who has to cry uncle.

"Hey, Armstrong," I say as he puts away the crib board. "Do you ever go ice fishing any more?"

He stops then smiles. Woohoo! That's two smiles (three if you count the invisible flying horse almost-smile) from him in two days, and his face didn't break. "Not any more. I'm old, I've got arthritis. But in the summer when it's warm, oh yes. There are a few channel cats left in that river that I need to speak to."

He sounds just like Peter. "Will you teach me?"

"Hmm. It depends." I get the laser eye treatment again. "It may not be worth my while. How long are you staying?"

Good question.

After lunch Armstrong takes some fresh rags to the barn (just for a change), and I decide to see if Peter is around. He is weirdly entertaining. I walk past the barn and the equipment sheds then climb down the bank to the river. Winter is over. There are lots of dark patches in the ice and even some open water, which reminds me of standing in the middle of a star, a memory I have to push to the back of my mind real quick. I don't see Peter at first but he's there, all right, sitting on a snow-drift with his back against the bank. This time I've brought a plastic bag. I spread it out and plunk down beside him.

"Hey."

"Hey, yourself. How's it goin'?"

That makes me smile. Peter is starting to talk like me.

"I'm bored. Whatcha doin'?"

Peter reaches down beside him to a sack that's sitting there. He pulls out a wicked looking knife. The blade is short and thin as if it's been sharpened a whole lot of times, enough to wear away some of the steel. But I can tell it's awesomely sharp. The handle's the best though. It looks like whoever made it glued thin pieces of different kinds of wood together before the handle was carved, so it's striped, dark and light. Peter probably made it himself because the grip fits his hand perfectly. He seems like the kind of guy who could do that sort of thing. Then he pulls out a hunk of wood and holds it up for me to see.

"Whoa!" I have never seen anything so cool.

"I'm making a catfish."

It's about fifty centimetres long, maybe more, and whittled out of a single piece of maple. The carving makes the channel cat look sinewy and strong, and the detail is amazing. The whiskers and the barbs (I don't know what they're really called) look scary and the fins are spiny and fierce. The heavy, flat head seems almost too big for the body, which Peter has carved in an undulating U shape just as if it is fighting a line. Most amazing of all is the skin. There are no scales, catfish don't have them, but Peter has somehow used the grain of the wood to give the skin dark and light patches just by how he's carved the wood.

"That is totally wicked, Peter," I say in awe. "How'd you ever learn to do that?"

"I've had lots of practice," he replies modestly.

I watch for a while as he rubs oil into the wood with a rag. From time to time he picks up the knife and makes some finishing touches. It's comfortable, just sitting and watching.

Although I wish I could do what he does. Man, this is better than anything I've ever seen in a gallery or a museum.

We sit so long it starts to get dark. And the bag keeps me dry but my butt freezes anyway. "I'd better go, Peter."

"Yes, you'd better," agrees Peter. He holds out the catfish. "Take this, Finn."

I go all still. No way. He can't mean that. It's like, a work of art. "I can't!"

"You have to, Finn." Peter puts the catfish into my hands, picks up his sack and starts to walk away. This time, though, he stops and looks over his shoulder at me. And he smiles.

I watch him walk away. He is one strange dude, that's all I can say. And there's something else weird. I can see my footprints in the snow. But I can't see his. What the heck is that about?

Holding the catfish carefully in one hand, I use the other to climb up the bank. There's a light in the barn but none in the kitchen, so Gran must be out. I put the catfish in the middle of the kitchen table then sit down and just look at it. I can't believe it's mine. It's not like I don't have good stuff of my own, books and electronics and sports equipment and all, but I don't own anything like this. Art. The kitchen's getting dark, but I don't want to put the light on because electricity just doesn't seem to belong in the same room as the catfish. A candle, that's what would work. Gran has one on the dining room table so I get it and light it and whoa – that channel cat is so beautiful. I love the way the light reflects in the oiled wood. It really glows.

There's a sudden draft and I have to cup my hands around the candle to stop it from going out. It's Armstrong, in from the barn. "Is the electricity off?" Then he sees the catfish.

"Where. Did. You. Get. That?" I look up, and Armstrong's face is absolutely white.

"My friend Peter gave it to me." I know there's going to have to be more explanation than that, and I open my mouth to start when Armstrong practically falls down. Good thing he falls in the direction of a chair because the fall's too sudden for me to stop it.

"How. Do. You. Know. Peter?"

So I tell him. But Armstrong is barely listening. He's just staring at the catfish. All of a sudden he snatches it and I yell, "Hey, that's mine!" But Armstrong just grabs my arm and hauls me outside into the snow. And he sure lives up to his name, I can tell you.

I start to ask him where he's taking me and I have to admit, I'm feeling a little nervous, but then I see that we're going to the barn. The barn. Finally.

He has to let go of my arm to get the key out of his pocket and that's okay by me because my arm is starting to hurt just a little. As I rub it, Armstrong struggles with the lock. He's so upset he can't open it, so I take the key, put it in the lock and then unwind the chain from the handles. But I don't open the door. That's for him to do.

Armstrong pushes the catfish back into my hands and opens the double doors. There's hardly any light left so he reaches into his pocket for some matches. He picks up an old-fashioned lantern that's right by the door and he lights it, then lifts it up over his head. My eyes follow the lantern, and I look up.

And I think my heart stops beating.

All the stalls and the hay and the equipment and everything

else you would expect to find in a barn are gone. There's no old car or motorcycle. It's just a big empty space. Empty except for the walls. The walls are lined with shelves and on those shelves are dozens – no, hundreds – of catfish just like mine.

The rich wood glows in the lantern light. There are dark ones and light ones, big ones and little ones. But they are clearly made by the same hand. The spiny fins and the sharp barbs, the play of dark and light, the way the bodies writhe, that's all the same. And there's a level of craftsmanship, that's what Mom would call it, that's unique. They're all just so *good*.

"Take this," Armstrong shoves the lantern into my hands and takes my catfish. "We have to compare."

I'm so overwhelmed I just do what I'm told. Armstrong is peering at the shelves. As I get closer, I see they're all numbered. "1950, where is 1950?" Armstrong is almost frantic. Then he finds it. He pulls the catfish labeled 1950 off its shelf and holds it close to my lantern. He compares 1950 with my catfish. Mine is bigger.

"Are there *any* fish bigger than yours? Any at all?" The lantern dances at the end of his arm as he scans all the carved fish. Armstrong's really scaring me. He grabs a stepladder and gestures frantically to a catfish high up on the wall.

"Get that one, the one up there!"

I do it, because I don't know what else to do. The number on this one is 1826. I climb down and show it to Armstrong. He makes me hold 1826 up to the two fish he's holding. 1826 is the biggest, but not by much.

"Oh, no," he whispers. His shoulders slump and his arms drop down to his sides, a catfish dangling from each hand.

"We're lost."

I don't know if you can even begin to imagine how confused I'm feeling now. And worried, too, about Armstrong. Has he completely lost it? I blow out the lantern, leave it by the door then push Armstrong out of the barn. Never mind the lock. I get him into the kitchen, take the three carved fish and set them on the table. I put the kettle on. Just then, Gran walks in and sees the catfish, then says something I totally don't expect.

"Oh, no," she says. "Not you too, Finn."

I stare at her.

"Not me too, what? I have no idea what's going on here, Gran, but Armstrong is freaking me out. Is he okay, or what?"

"He'll be all right. Just surprised. I assume you've met Peter?"

"Well, yeah, but why's that a big deal? I want to know about all the catfish in the barn!"

"It's Armstrong's story, really. Armstrong met Peter when he was about your age."

"Different Peter, Gran. My Peter is only about thirty."

Armstrong rouses himself. "Same Peter. My father knew him, and his father and his father. Only Armstrong who didn't was your father."

"That's crazy. Who carved all the fish?"

"Peter. Did he tell you about the flood he and his family went through?"

"Yeaaah," I say slowly.

"It was in 1826, and Peter nearly died in that flood. An Armstrong rescued him. His people, the Swiss, gave up on the settlement after that and moved south, but the Scots stayed. And Peter stayed too, because he was too badly hurt to travel. He married an Armstrong and they were happy, but the very next year cholera came to the settlement and Peter died. But he didn't leave. Every year since then, Peter has carved a catfish and given it to an Armstrong. The size of the catfish matches the size of the flood to come so we can prepare."

I can't believe what I'm hearing. I've got to slow it down. After about ten deep breaths I say, "You're saying Peter is a ghost with a built-in early warning system?"

"He's never wrong," says Armstrong. "The scientists make all sorts of predictions, but Mother Nature sometimes stymies them anyway. Peter is *never* wrong," he repeats just to make sure I get it. "The fact that he's a ghost doesn't matter. The question is how do we prepare? Your catfish is bigger than the 1950 catfish and that was one of the worst floods ever. The 1826 catfish is just a little bigger than yours and that was the flood that not only destroyed the entire settlement, but almost took away any hope of there even *being* a settlement, ever at all!" Armstrong's hair is looking wild and crazy again, like Dad's. He's really upset.

So am I. The fact that I've been talking to a two-hundred-year-old ghost and I didn't even know *doesn't matter?* Oh yes, it does. Big time.

Armstrong wants to start warning people about the flood right that minute, and he's yelling and fighting with Gran. He's kind of scary to watch because his hair's all crackly and his face is red and crumply, and if he wasn't so old he'd be jumping around like a pogo stick. Gran's not having much luck calming him down. I just leave. I need time to process. Armstrong's a really old man and as much as he looks sane, no doubt he's lost a few brain cells. There could be a bunch of explanations for the catfish and for Peter that steer way clear of a horror story. Maybe Armstrong carved all the catfish and Peter is just his imaginary friend or something. Except that makes him my imaginary friend too, and up until today I didn't think I was crazy. And even worse, Gran is just too calm. And she definitely isn't crazy.

I go to my room, boot up the Internet and type in "Peter de Meuron." There aren't any hits on him exactly, but there are lots on "de Meuron" in general. It was the name of a regiment of mercenary soldiers in the 1700s, named after its commander, Charles-Daniel de Meuron from Switzerland. Swiss mercenary soldiers, now who would guess that? The regiment was hired by the Dutch to fight in South Africa and later, hired by the British to come to Canada and fight in the War of 1812. After that was over, Lord Selkirk, the guy who started the colony in the Red River Valley, hired them. Lord Selkirk needed them to help protect the settlers. He gave them land grants close to the Forks, and they sent for their families. The Swiss settlement was called St. Boniface. But after the flood of 1826, the Swiss threw in the towel and left. Thanks, Google.

All the pieces of the story fit. But no way can it be true.

Finally Gran talks Armstrong into going to bed. She looks really tired but I have to talk to her or I won't be able to sleep. The kettle shut itself off ages ago, but I turn it back on and make a couple of sandwiches and take everything out to the living room where she's sitting.

"So, what gives, Gran? Does he have Alzheimer's or something?"

She gives me a tiny smile. "No, he's perfectly sane."

I wait.

"I've known about Peter since before I was married. Just before the wedding your grandfather came to me and said he had to tell me a family secret. He had to tell me right then so I had a chance to back out of the marriage if I wanted. The story, the one you just heard, sounded as crazy to me as it does to you. Your grandfather believed it though, and said that when we were married we had to live on the farm so we could carry on with Peter now that Armstrong was growing older. I went along with it because I loved your grandfather very much. I thought that in time, he would see that the story was just the imaginings of an old man.

"But your grandfather died and Armstrong didn't. One spring, I followed Armstrong to the riverbank and hid. There was nobody there. Armstrong talked away to thin air and I was sure he was a little touched. But then out of nowhere a catfish appeared. I couldn't see from where. Armstrong took the catfish, climbed up the bank and went to the barn. The next day he called the men of the village and sandbagging began.

"I can't explain it, Finn, especially to a budding scientist," Gran gave me another gentle smile. "But I've come to believe that some things can't be explained in this world, at least, not yet. Maybe sometime in the future science will be able to make sense of such mysteries. But in the meantime I simply have to allow myself to live with unanswered questions. And if you can actually see Peter, you'll have to learn to do the same."

"No way."

Gran pats me on the arm and goes upstairs to bed. The tea is cold, and the sandwiches are untouched.

CHAPTER 7

The Flood Club

April 1997

I've entered some kind of twilight zone, an alternate reality maybe. Armstrong won't let go of this idea that Peter is a ghost, or that my catfish has predicted a monster flood. He even called some men and they're all coming over to the house to talk about it. How can you discuss something like this?

"Do these men know you have your own personal ghost?" I sound sarcastic. Aaron would be proud.

Armstrong practically snarls back, "Of course not."

Gran's reply is milder. "People around here just think that the Armstrong family has a sixth sense about the floods."

Armstrong says we can't talk about Peter to anybody because it will make us sound crazy. You think? But we still have to let everybody know that there's a huge flood coming. I say, no problem. There are a million scientists watching the river, but they're all going to believe an old codger who just *knows*.

When the men come they're all looking pretty serious. I hang out in the kitchen to eavesdrop.

"How bad?" That's from the man who looks like the leader. Okay, so I'm peeking as well as eavesdropping.

"Worse than 1950."

The man swears quietly. "All right, I'm on it. Thanks, Armstrong."

Then another man snorts with laughter. "This again? Surely you're not going to believe the ravings of an old man?"

The leader stares the other man down. "I sure am. He knows what he's talking about."

The second man just laughs. Then he says some really ugly things about Armstrong. It's a pretty sure bet that Armstrong's crazy, but that guy doesn't have to be mean about it. He reminds me of Fred, and he's starting to make me angry. Armstrong's been around for a long time, you know; it's not like he's a complete idiot. I'm beginning to understand why Armstrong is "famous," but I don't like that this guy's making him look like a fool.

You know I'm only saying these things in my head, right? But there *is* one thing I can do to stop him. I step into the doorway so everybody can see me. This is a trick you should remember. Grown-ups get embarrassed when kids hear the stupid things they say. It's as if all of a sudden the adults start hearing themselves, and they don't like what they hear, so they stop. Works like a charm.

The guy stops. There are some sighs and some grumbles, and then all the men start to make plans that involve truckloads of sand, plastic bags and shovels. The leader believes Armstrong. That's all that matters. One of the men pulls out a map and they start drawing lines on it. Then Gran serves cookies and they go home. Armstrong is all happy now, but I'm not. I mean, just because I don't like hearing awful things about Armstrong doesn't mean I believe his story. I can't.

When Dad gets this way about his research, he goes to the gym and lifts weights. You can stop laughing now. He's not trying to bulk up, he's trying to numb out. Dad says that exercise tires him out to the point that his mind goes blank. He can't think of anything, except how tired he is. And after he rests and thoughts flow back into his brain, they come back in a different order. Sometimes that's enough to help him solve the problem.

I wonder if there's a gym around here. Although Dad's technique might not solve problems that come from the twilight zone.

At supper, I take a deep breath. "I'm not saying that I buy this ghost story. But those men believed you about the flood. So what's going to happen?"

"Sandbag. That's all anybody can do."

"What do you mean, sandbag?"

Armstrong just looks at me. Gran is the one who explains. "We fill bags with sand, then use the bags to build a wall to hold the water back."

"You mean, build a wall around the house?"

"We mean," says Armstrong, "build a wall around every house in the valley." He says this in a way that makes me think he's really saying, "What kind of a nincompoop are you?"

But I really don't get it. "Isn't that an awful lot of sandbags?"

Armstrong doesn't even bother to answer me.

"Who fills them all?"

This question, he answers. "You do."

Oh.

Somehow I feel that this is all my fault, since it was my catfish that started it. So when the sand and bags and everything that the men have ordered arrive, I accidentally on purpose miss the school bus. Crazy or not, I have to stick with it. First thing in the morning, Gran drops both me and Armstrong on Main Street. I'm amazed at the number of people there, most of the men in the village I guess, as well as a bunch of farmers I don't recognize. I don't know if they all believe Armstrong or if they believe the men that came to our house, but for sure my catfish started something big.

The plan is to build a wall – a dike – around the whole village. Other villages have permanent dikes but not Ste. Agathe because it's already on high ground and doesn't ever flood. Well, hardly ever. I can't imagine how much water it would take for the river to spill its banks here, but the men have worked it all out. They know how many sandbags they need and where the dike is going to go. There's nothing left to do but get started.

Newbies, like me, get to fill bags. It's not hard, you just pour sand into a bag. But then you have to toss the bag to your neighbour, who tosses it to his neighbour, who tosses it to his neighbour – you get it? And these bags are heavy, about twenty kilos. The guy at the end of the line builds the dike by laying the sandbags on top of each other. And that's it.

It doesn't take long to get a rhythm going. Armstrong's in charge of engineering. He's apparently an expert dike-builder and they need his expertise. Why am I not surprised? Anyway, he's way too old to toss sandbags. So far, the weather is spring-like and you can see the snowdrifts melting into the storm sewers. I'm thinking that if enough of the snow melts, maybe we won't have a flood. But maybe not. I let my mind wander. I really want to numb out. For the record, filling sandbags is a really good way to do that.

We change places on the line. Fillers become tossers, and tossers become fillers. There's no doubt I'm getting the workout I asked for, but in future I think I'll be more careful what I wish for. My elbows hurt. After a couple of hours, I see Gran driving the truck back, and I smell cookies. All right! More trucks come with more ladies and more food, sandwiches, fruit and coffee and stuff. Everybody stops for lunch, and I think to myself, This is a tonne of fun. It really is. Hard, but fun. After lunch we change positions again, except at one point, Armstrong comes to get me out of the line and takes me to the dike because he wants me to watch how it's built. The first thing I see is a bunch of men digging a trench about fifteen centimetres deep and forty-five centimetres across. This is to anchor the centre of the dike before the sandbags are put on top of it. Then Armstrong shows me how the bags fit together, overlapping like bricks in a wall. The dike is about twice as wide at the bottom as it is at the top. And the height of the dike, well, that's all up to a guy in Winnipeg named Alf Warkentin. He's a hydrometeorologist (another - ologist) and is responsible for forecasting the height of the flood. All the dike-builders listen to him to figure out how high their dikes have to be, then everybody prays that he got it right. Not a job I'd want, thank you very much. How would you feel if hundreds of thousands of people were depending on your math?

If you have time after the sandbags are in position, you

cover the bags with plastic because that helps stop erosion. You don't want the water to eat its way between the bags and cause a breach. And if you think it's going to be windy, then you put a boom on the water side of the dike, kind of like the ones they use when there's an oil spill, to help stop the waves from pounding your dike and breaking it up.

When I think I've got it, Armstrong takes me back to the line for more filling and tossing, only now I'm feeling more like an engineer than a brute force labourer. A dike is so simple and so complicated at the same time.

By the end of the day we have a dike up to my shoulders about thirty metres long and I wonder how many sandbags are in it. When I ask, somebody says we filled nine thousand sandbags. All that for thirty metres? Ste. Agathe isn't big, but we must have at least a couple of kilometres to go, and I, for one, am already exhausted.

But not exhausted enough to stop thinking about Peter.

Gran won't let me miss the school bus again. Clara practically jumps me as soon as I get off the bus.

"Where were you yesterday?"

"Busy," I say.

Clara stares at me curiously. "Too busy for school?"

"It's kind of a long story," I say. Just then Hazel and Jane show up.

"You know what I heard?" says Hazel. "They're already sandbagging in Ste. Agathe. They think there's going to be a really big flood this year."

"Why?" asks Jane. "There haven't been any flood announcements yet."

"No, but Ste. Agathe always seems to know before anybody else," she says. "Remember there was that article in the paper last year about it? People think they've got a crystal ball or something."

Aaron and Roy come round the corner. Roy's humming the theme from The Twilight Zone. He really likes to hum. This time he has no idea how right he is. "I guess that means you come from the weird side of the tracks, buddy."

As I brace myself for his shoulder punch, I wonder what he'd say if he really knew. "Hey folks, it's not a crystal ball, it's a wooden catfish." Nope, they're not going to hear it from me.

"Are they really, Finn? Sandbagging, I mean?" asks Clara. "Is that what you were doing?"

"Yeah," I say. "It was hard work, but kind of fun. There's a lot more to do though." Clara frowns. I can almost see wheels turning in her brain. Then she looks at me and her eyes are all sparkly. "What?"

"I have a great idea!" she says. "We should start a Flood Club. We can ask Ned to be our teacher sponsor. We'll get everybody organized into sandbagging teams and we'll build dikes wherever we're needed. We'll start in Ste. Agathe. It'll be totally cool."

Aaron just lifts that eyebrow of his. "Newsflash – the river floods every year. A little or a lot, it doesn't matter, the Red rises every year. And we're covered. We've got dikes everywhere. Don't sweat it."

But Clara's on a roll. "But what if this one is really big? I mean, if Ste. Agathe has already started sandbagging they must think it's going to be bad. Most years they don't bag at all. And if it's big, they're going to need us." I can tell she's getting excited.

Aaron shakes his head. "Aren't you just a knight in shining armour, come to save the day! Or would that be a princess?"

"Shut up," says Clara. "At least I come up with the occasional interesting idea."

"A Flood Club?" asks Hazel. "I don't get it."

"Don't the adults do that, build dikes and stuff? Don't you have to be an engineer or a fireman or something?" asks Jane.

"Do we get to wear capes?" asks Roy. "Floooooooodfighters!" He punches his fist into the air and everybody laughs.

"It's not funny," insists Clara. "They're going to need *everybody* to help build the dikes. Why shouldn't we help? Finn helped yesterday." She looks over at me.

She might be on to something. We only did a little bit yesterday. I don't know when the flood is coming, but there's a lot more sandbagging to do.

"I like it," I say. "More people would be better."

"And you honestly think they'll let kids do this?" Hazel says.

"They're going to have to," says Clara firmly.

It's Aaron's turn to frown. "You know, you might be right. People always underestimate what kids can do. We should show them." I have to check his face to see if he's just getting on Clara's case, but it looks like he really means it. I totally get why Aaron thinks that way, but I'm kind of wondering if he can even be a floodfighter. I mean, there's the whole wheelchair thing. Aaron looks at me, and I know he knows what I'm thinking. Suddenly his arms come up from his lap and he throws an invisible sandbag in my direction.

"Here, catch!"

What he's doing looks so real I reach out my arms to catch it and instinctively stagger back a step because I can almost feel the weight of the imaginary bag. "My arms work just fine," he says quietly.

So does his brain. "Done," I say. I stick my fist out. "Here's to the Flood Club." Clara puts her hand on mine. Aaron puts his hand on Clara's. The others jump up from their seats and grab on to our hands. "Flooooodfighters!"

Clara's hand is really soft.

Ned is enthusiastic; there may even be extra credit in it for us. He says we have to have a mission statement, a budget, a membership drive and a plan of action to be a club. We all go to Clara's house after school to organize.

The mission statement is pretty easy: "The mission of the Flood Club is to help fight the upcoming flood." I'm in charge of writing things down.

"Shouldn't it be more poetic?" asks Jane. "I mean, if this is going to be a really epic flood, shouldn't our mission be grander? Something like this: 'The mission of the Flood Club is to be like modern-day Noahs who hold back the rising sea, protect property from cataclysmic destruction and rescue innocent victims from the raging waters of the Red River.'"

We all just look at her. Finally Roy says, "But Noah didn't hold back the sea. He let everything flood. All he did was protect a few animals."

"And that's exactly what we're going to do. The river is supposed to flood, we're just going to protect the stuff that's in the way. Like Ste. Agathe," Clara replies firmly.

"I like Jane's mission statement best," says Hazel. "Me too," chimes in Roy. I roll my eyes.

"Whatever. What do we need to budget for?" We make a list. Floodfighters are going to need rubber boots and heavy gloves. We need transportation to get to sandbagging centres. We decide that we can hit our parents up for rides and most of us have rubber boots already. That leaves gloves.

"I've got it!" says Clara. "We'll do a fundraiser for the gloves. A dance. Five bucks a ticket and the money goes to buy gloves. Maybe we can even get a DJ to come for free and the grocery store to donate pop and chips. Then, once we have the gloves, we do the membership drive. You join, you get gloves."

"Excellent." I'm scribbling furiously. "Now for the plan of action. First, we need to divide the membership up into teams and set up a parental taxi service. Then, we need to have a number for people to call if they need our help. Do you think we can get the paper to advertise our services?"

"Shouldn't we learn how to sandbag first?" More sarcasm from Aaron.

I grin. "Goes without saying; Armstrong can help us with that."

"It doesn't go without saying, you numbskull." Aaron grins back at me. "That's the hardest part. Write it down." So I do. I'm feeling kind of stoked about this whole idea.

It's Wednesday already. Floods wait for no one, so the dance has to be this Friday. Ned gets all the permissions for us, Aaron and Jane go after the local stores for pop and stuff, and Roy says he's got a cousin who can DJ for free (I'm a little worried about that). Hazel even goes after donated pizza. Clara and I work on advertising, and this turns out to be the hardest job. It's no problem getting the student body to come to a dance, especially a dance with free pizza. But flood fundraising? Nobody cares. Now I'm really feeling like Noah. Why won't they listen? There's no point in buying gloves if nobody will wear them.

Clara and I put our heads together at lunch on Thursday. "It's not that they don't want to help, everybody will if the water comes close. But since the last flood there's been so much effort go into building dikes that everybody thinks the problem is solved," sighs Clara. "Somehow we have to make rubber boots and gloves cool."

And that's when I start to smile, because I know just how to do it.

For a while, I went to school in South Africa while my parents studied the Orange River. And in South Africa, people dance in rubber boots. There are a lot of gold mines in South Africa, and the working conditions in the mines used to be pretty bad. The mines regularly filled up with water. Instead of draining the mineshafts they way they should have, the mine owners made all the workers wear rubber boots to protect their feet so they wouldn't get sick. This was during the time of *apartheid*, when the white South Africans treated black people really badly. Black workers couldn't even talk while they were working or they'd lose their jobs. So instead of talking, the workers tapped out rhythms on their boots in a kind of code. They stomped and clapped and hit their boots, and it became a way of communicating without words. The guards never caught on.

Nowadays all that stomping and clapping is called gumboot dancing. And that is how we are going to make rubber boots cool.

The night of the dance I'm feeling a little nervous. If my gumboot dance falls flat, I will be the joke of the whole school. It's probably a good thing that I don't actually live here because long-term embarrassment could be involved. But so far, so good. The turnout is great, thanks to the pizza. At five bucks a head, we've already made a lot of money on tickets alone. Roy's cousin isn't too awful, and everybody seems to be having a good time. I really want to dance with Clara, but we're both too busy. Maybe later. We wait about an hour until things are really rocking then shut down the music. There are a few catcalls, but mostly the dancers are confused. The principal gets up and gives a little speech about the fundraising campaign and about how important it is to be prepared for the flood, and, wonder of wonders, he keeps it to the five minutes we gave him. Now it's our turn. The Flood Club takes a collective breath and goes out on stage.

At first everybody laughs but we're expecting that. We're all wearing work coveralls stuffed into rubber boots, and hard hats. Wouldn't you laugh? Even Aaron is on stage because you can clap your hands and hit your boots just fine from a wheelchair. I start to chant out the rhythms then we all start stamping our feet in time. Then it's a kick to the back, side step, low kick and hop. And again. Gumboot dancing is easy, really just line dancing with a way better beat. We keep stomping out the rhythm and pretty soon the rest of the kids are clapping along. It's working! Some people start to stomp and the really brave ones come up on stage with us. It's a hoot, and everybody's having fun.

And the best part? When we figure it's time, we take off our boots and pass them around. And just like that our fundraising campaign gets kicked into high gear.

On Saturday Clara and her mom take the money and buy the gloves, and they get a deal so there's even enough money left to buy T-shirts with FLOOD CLUB printed on them. Then Mrs. Taylor brings the Flood Club to my house. Gran makes a boatload of cookies and it feels like a party until Armstrong comes in from the barn. The rest of them haven't met him before so he's a bit of a shock, kind of like a mini Rumpelstiltskin daring the flood to come and get him. He lectures us on bagging and dike-building and on the forces of nature and he's actually inspiring in a scary sort of way. Roy looks totally terrified. By the time Armstrong's done with us, we know what we have to do. The Flood Club is going to hold back the rising sea.

CHAPTER 8

The Beginning

It's hard to say what the post-dance mood is going to be. What I don't expect is a new school trend, but that's exactly what happens. Flood gear becomes the new fashion statement. I'm not kidding. Madison and her crew show up at school on Monday, wearing work coveralls stuffed into rubber boots. Their names are written on the back of the coveralls in sequins. Ugh. Tuesday, Elizabeth's gang has painted pink flowers on their boots with nail polish, and they're wearing dollar-store hard hats decorated with plastic flowers. And it's not just the girls, the guys are wearing rubber boots (no flowers) too. Gumboot dances are breaking out in the hallways. It's amazing. Inevitably, somebody shows up wearing a floodfighter cape. Roy is thrilled. And in the end, we get what we wanted. Almost everybody signs up for Flood Club. All I can hope is that we really are going to have the flood of the century because if we don't, Flood Club will just be a bad joke. But I don't think we'll get that lucky.

About seventy kids sign up to come to Ste. Agathe on the weekend, and the principal arranges for school buses to bring them all over, which is great. I let Gran know and she and her ladies start making plans for LOTS of sandwiches. By Saturday afternoon the dike is curving around the end of Main Street, and we are just like a machine; bag, toss, bag, toss, bag, toss. We're a sea of bright red T-shirts standing hip to hip, passing the bags from hand to hand, and I've never had so much fun. I guess it's like being on a sports team (not that I ever have), except you're not trying to beat your friends. You're trying to beat Mother Nature, and it feels, well, like Jane said. Epic.

By late Saturday afternoon, snowflakes are falling from the sky. Even though the weather's been nice we knew a storm was coming, because now that we're officially on flood watch, everybody's been pretty glued to the weather station. It's a storm out of the Rockies, via Colorado, and it's supposed to be bad, although it's hard to imagine how a storm in Colorado can be a problem for Winnipeg. We quit bagging a little early, partly because everybody's muscles are screaming and partly so the school buses can get back to Easthaven before the storm gets too bad. And does it get bad.

All day Sunday we are shut inside. The snow keeps coming and the wind is ferocious. Armstrong's pretty much bouncing off the walls he's so anxious. He's even worse than me. I get out the crib board, but I beat Armstrong game after game, he's just not concentrating. In all, fifty centimetres of snow falls on top of the hundred and fifty or so that we already had. As far as Armstrong is concerned, it's nothing short of a disaster.

He's not alone. By Monday, the six o'clock news is all about the coming "big one." They're calling this weekend's snow-storm a "Colorado Clipper," and scientists say it's the last straw.

All the elements are in place for the flood of the century. Forecasters announce there's going to be more water than 1979 and even 1950. There might be more water than any flood since 1861. Yeah, tell me something I don't already know. The Armstrong men can read catfish.

Alf Warkentin, our hydrometeorologist, talks the government into hiring the U.S. Weather Service to overfly the valley, using their fancy equipment to measure ground radiation, because from that, he can tell the water content of the snow. They say yes, because Warkentin's the man. He gets the results, works the numbers and figures out the height of the crest, which is the highest point of the flood as it passes through a town. The news isn't good. Warkentin says the river is going to crest way higher than previously thought; higher than a lot of the dikes.

We're officially in deep trouble.

Even though we can hardly get out of our own house and the temperature is way below freezing, there's no time to waste. Armstrong's on the phone with some of the men from the village and within days, Ste. Agathe is flooded, not by water but by soldiers. Three hundred of them show up, and in no time the ring dike is finished. I didn't think I was stressed about the fact that the farm wasn't protected, but I must have been because now I feel relieved. The soldiers move on to St. Adolphe, and so do we. The Flood Club is open for new business.

Now that the government has released its flood predictions, everyone gets into sandbagging. Since we were first, the *Winnipeg Free Press* decides to put the Flood Club in the news. Clara calls everybody to come for a photo shoot, and I'm surprised that she's called Fred too.

"Why's he here?"

"It's my special powers," she says, but I still don't get it. She tells him we need somebody who looks strong to throw a sandbag and he's okay with it. The newspaper photographer takes a picture of a bunch of us passing sandbags along the line, with Fred at the end tossing one into the back of his dad's pickup truck. We tell the reporter we're ready for action, and the calls start coming in as soon as the paper's out. Everybody needs us. Fred struts around the school, convinced it is his manly body that all the callers want. Whatever. A waste of special powers if you ask me, but at least he signs up for Flood Club. A bunch of moms, including Gran, come to school and use the staff room to organize the teams and buses. Some teams are assigned to the school to fill bags, others will be sent out to farms to build dikes and others will load trucks. There'll be work enough for everybody, but right now we have to wait for the bags and the sand to arrive. When they do, it's hard to stay in class. Every spare moment, we all race outside to the parking lot to fill sandbags. A bunch of Flood Club members cut class. During morning announcements, the principal says that students are to be reminded that this is not a holiday. Funny, it kind of feels that way. The only class we don't cut is geography. Ned has this big map, and we're going to plot the path of the flood. Flood Stop #1 is Fargo, North Dakota.

There's panic in Fargo. The American scientists estimate that the river will crest in Fargo a foot and a half higher than their levees, which is what the Americans call dikes. The people of Fargo sandbag like crazy, but in the end, the water crests at a foot and a half below the levees. The scientists blame a malfunctioning river flow monitor for the bad estimate, but nobody cares; the city is safe.

Flood Stop #2 is Grand Forks, North Dakota. They've got a week before the crest gets to them and they're feeling optimistic. A week later, the crest will cross the Canadian border and we have to be ready.

Flood Stop #3 is Emerson, Manitoba. Two weeks. It's not much time.

Today we go south toward Emerson. The town has a permanent dike, but the farmers outside the town are responsible for their own dikes. A lot of them already have bags and sand. They just need us to put it all together. The bus drops us off, we take our positions, the baggers start, and the minute the first bag is filled the rhythm begins. There are no trucks here so we build as we bag. Bag, toss, position, bag, toss, position. Sometimes we sing. At first I don't even know who owns this farm, not that it matters, but I figure it out when we stop for a break. The supervisor of our team talks to an elderly man about where the dike should go. The property is spread out just like our farm, with a barn and some equipment sheds a little way off from the house. I can see the two men pointing and in the end they mark out a path that includes the house but not the outbuildings.

I think to myself that I've just watched a guy decide to abandon his barn and all his outbuildings because it would take more sandbags than he has. His wife is serving coffee and I see the farmer catch her eye. The wife turns away, and her shoulders start to shake a bit. I think she's crying.

The next few days pass in a blur of sandbag brigades. Every morning we get ourselves to the high-school parking lot to get sorted into teams. There are red shirts everywhere. Word has spread about Flood Club, so when people see the red shirts coming two things usually happen. First, they ask us to do a gumboot dance and second, they have cookies waiting. It's kind of becoming our thing.

The news from upstream isn't good. Grand Forks is in big trouble. The flood is nearly there and the levees aren't high enough. The river has grown to fourteen kilometres wide and parts of the city are already under water. So far the main levees in the downtown area are holding, but nobody knows for how long.

And then the flood will hit Emerson, Flood Stop #3. The Canadian military just got there to help build the dikes higher. The soldiers are kind of like the flood, with more and more flowing in every day. Seeing them makes me feel like I'm in a war zone instead of Canada. The soldiers are pretty nice though. Armstrong, Gran and I watch the news every night after supper, and tonight there are pictures of huge army-truck convoys loaded with sandbags. A ton of work went into filling them. Believe me, I am in a position to know. After the news, Armstrong and I get out the crib board. It's fourteen games to twelve, Armstrong's ahead.

It's Saturday morning and every member of the Flood Club is at the school as soon as the sun is up. All teams, red shirts on, are ready for deployment. We're like a machine and I feel so proud. But the whole system grinds to a halt when the principal, who's wearing a red shirt and rubber boots just like the rest of us, rolls out a TV set. He turns on the news, but it's more like watching a horror movie. All I can see through the crowd (why do tall people always stand at the front?) is a bunch of buildings in the middle of a lake. They're all on fire and huge flames are shooting into the air. It looks like the way they describe hell, except it's not. That "lake" is the Red River. And the flames? That's Grand Forks, or at least what's left of it.

This is what they say happened: when the people saw how high the river was getting, the whole city frantically tried to add more height to their levees. The only way to build higher fast enough was to bulldoze earth on top of the levees but loose dirt doesn't have much holding power. The dike-builders just didn't have enough time to pack it down, and one by one, the levees failed. The Red River crashed into downtown, filling all the streets, basements and shops. The electricity shorted out, and the gas pipelines ruptured. A huge fire started downtown that nobody could put out. Firefighters couldn't get close to the blaze. Building after building caught fire and burned. Too much water and not enough, all at the same time.

The newscaster says that thirty-five thousand of the fifty-two thousand people who live in Grand Forks are homeless. They sandbagged right up until the end, but it was all for nothing.

That's not going to happen to us.

We have one more week, a week that Grand Forks didn't have. There's nothing like seeing disaster to inspire your work ethic. The principal gives us an unnecessary pep talk, and everybody heads to the sand piles. Aaron's already there, throwing those sandbags as if they were nothing. I had no idea he was that strong. I try to keep up. When I go faster, he goes faster. When he goes faster, I go faster. Pretty soon we're laughing like crazy.

After a while, some of us get loaded onto a bus and taken to somebody's farm. Get this. I'm now the most experienced sandbagger in this group, so I get to be the supervisor. Unbelievable. The farmer tells me where the dike is going to go and I have to make sure the bags are packed so they'll hold. It's really cold, and the rest of his family is inside. There are two little kids watching through the living-room window. When Armstrong showed me how to build a dike, it looked easy. Now I'm not so sure. What if I get it wrong? What if those little kids lose their house?

The news today says that the mayor of Winnipeg has ordered a million more sandbags. A million, and that's on top of the million they already had. And here I thought nine thousand was a lot. The mayor did it because Alf Warkentin said the river's going even higher and it's thrown the city into a tizzy. At least Winnipeg has two Sandbaggers – octopus-type machines that can fill twelve bags at once. I wouldn't mind one of those. But lots of people in the city say there's really no need to worry. "Have no fear, the floodway is here." Actually, I think they're right. We are so on top of it.

A good thing happened on the line today. I'm getting to know a lot of the volunteers in this area, so I was surprised when a new kid got on the bus. I asked him what school he was from, and it turns out he's from Ontario. He used his newspaper route money, with a little help from his parents and grandparents, to come all by himself to sandbag. It was amazing.

"Why?" I asked him.

"Because it's the weekend and at home all I'd be doing would be playing video games. Because I've got strong arms and you guys shouldn't have to do all the work. Because they're calling this the flood of the century and I want to be part of it."

Yeah, I get it.

But a bad thing happened today too. A little boy died. He was only four and the flood swept him into a ditch.

There's lots of news today:

First, Duff Roblin, the guy who got the floodway built, threw the switch that opens the floodway gates and it's a week earlier than planned. The crest still hasn't crossed the border but the one thing you can't do with a flood is let it get ahead of you. And even with the floodway, Winnipeg is raising its permanent dikes by two feet. Next, the Princess Patricia's Canadian Light Infantry have arrived. They're not helping yet. Instead, they're training people about stuff like electrocution, hypothermia and near-drowning injuries. Fun, fun, fun. Third, the government has started evacuating people upstream. Fourth, helicopters are dumping sand on the ice in the river, trying to thaw it as fast as possible so it won't jam. And fifth, we've run out of sandbags.

But none of that is the real news. You know that story of the boy who finds a hole in a dike and sticks his finger in it to save his whole country? We've got one of those. This guy named Richardson who works for the Highways Department is looking at a map and he sees a hole in the dike, a big one. It's called the La Salle River. The way he figures it, the flood is going to be so big that the water's going to flow overland into the La Salle River, which is a tributary of the Red. And the La Salle will flow it right back into the Red inside the floodway and inside the dikes. Goodbye, Winnipeg. The Highways Department is going berserk. This guy didn't just put his finger into it, he put his whole head.

CHAPTER 9

Armstrong

I feel exhausted and exhilarated at the same time. The flood has taken over everything, not just for me, but for everybody in the valley. There is no normal routine any more. You remember I said that seventy people signed up for Flood Club? That's nothing. We were just the first, thanks to Peter. Now there are ten thousand people on sandbagging duty. Kids are filling bags, teachers are building dikes, office workers are checking for leaks, farmers have sent all their animals away and are parking their combines and tractors on the highest roads they can find. We all watch the news every night and worry together. There's even a special channel just for flood information called Plugged In! I feel bad when I say it's fun, but it is. It's epic.

The bus drops me off and I drag myself up the lane. I love feeling this tired. Too bad I'm an Armstrong though, because all this work is just making me skinnier. Fred, on the other hand, can't stop showing off his new muscles. Hopefully he won't use them to beat anybody up. Aaron's growing muscles too, but not just in his arms. He's stopped being sarcastic all the time. He works the line like everybody else, so all the people who used to feel sorry for him have stopped. And he's a great organizer. The volunteers depend on him to figure out who should do what because he always puts the right people in the right place. I think things are going to be different for him when this is all over. I mean, it's not like he didn't have friends before. But the way they're friends is going to change. I kind of wish that I was staying long enough to see how that plays out.

There's no light on in the kitchen so I use my key and go into a cold, quiet house. There's no dinner in the fridge. Gran must be late. I'd start something but the kitchen is her domain and nobody messes with it if they can help it. I'm about to turn on the news when the phone rings. It's a neighbour from down the street. I've met her a couple of times, mostly because she makes the best sandwiches. I keep my eye open for her at lunchtime. When I decided to call her creations "sandbag subs" she laughed.

"Finn, are you home?"

"Sure, Mrs. St. Pierre, I'm sitting in the living room." (Where the phone is, duh.)

"Get your coat on, I'm coming over to pick you up."

I can tell from her voice that something's wrong. "What's going on?"

"It's Armstrong. We told him and told him that he was too old for another flood. He's earned the right for others to take care of him for a change. We told him."

"Mrs. St. Pierre, what happened? What happened to Armstrong?" I'm almost yelling.

"He had a heart attack. They rushed him to the hospital in Winnipeg and your Gran went with him. I promised I'd bring you as soon as you got home."

OMG. Armstrong. Gran must be frantic. "I'm getting my coat on right now. Come! Come!" I shout at poor Mrs. St. Pierre.

I pester her like crazy for the first ten kilometres, but all she knows is the name of the hospital and that Armstrong was conscious when they put him in the ambulance. For the rest of the ride we're both quiet. I'm scared. Even after the dike was finished, Armstrong just wouldn't quit. He was organizing teams of volunteers to check for leaks and add more height. He was never home, he was always at the dike, yelling at people.

Mrs. St. Pierre says she'll come in with me so she can check with Gran about whether or not we'll need a ride home. If Gran wants to stay in Winnipeg she knows a good hotel. I'm hardly listening and just want the elevator to move faster. I pretty much fly out of it when the doors open, and then I race to the nurse's station. They tell me the room number and I start walking — real slow. Now that I'm here I don't want to be.

I peek in the room. Gran sees me and comes out into the hallway, closing the door behind her.

"It's all right, Finn. He's going to be all right. He's sleeping right now, which is exactly what he needs to do. The doctor said it was surprisingly minor for a ninety-four-year-old man and that he'll be up in no time."

"For real?"

"For real."

"Honest?"

"Honest."

"Armstrong's ninety-four?" Gran just smiles.

"Caroline?" comes a weak voice through the door.

"Sleeping, huh?" I give her a wry smile. "Can I go in?"

"Sure."

I tiptoe in. I'm not used to hospitals, thank goodness. Armstrong looks pretty bad to me, all grey in the face and sort of trembly, not like him at all. And the machines don't help, blinking and beeping each heartbeat away. If I were Gran I wouldn't trust that doctor, but then what do I know? Maybe everybody looks like this after a heart attack.

"Hey, Armstrong," I say as I reach the bed. He puts out his hand and reaches for me. I've never touched anybody as old as Armstrong before. His hand feels thin and dry and papery, not strong at all. I try to hold it gently. "How do you feel?"

"How do you think?" he asks sarcastically, and I have to smile. Maybe that doctor's right after all. "What are you doing here?"

"Being with you," I answer. "You need us."

"I need her," he says, pointing at Gran. "She takes care of me, not you. You've got better things to do."

"Calm yourself, Armstrong," says Gran. "You got everybody bagging early, so there are lots of people to do the work. You've done your part."

"But he should be there! He has to learn!" splutters Armstrong, pointing at me. "What good's he going to do here, playing nursemaid to an antique like me? He's young, he's strong and the line needs him!"

"Sh," Gran says softly. "He's only one boy. There are thousands out there working the line. Finn and I will stay in Winnipeg tonight so we can be close. We'll go back tomorrow."

"No!" Armstrong shouts so loud the nurse comes in to check him. "He's an Armstrong. He should be out there. Bad enough I'm here. Send him home."

"He's too young to stay by himself."

"Too young! When I was a boy…" Gran and I both start to laugh.

"Gran," I say, "he's not going to be a very good patient."

"No kidding," she laughs.

"I am old enough, you know," I tell Gran. "All I'm going to do is sleep, eat breakfast, and get picked up again tomorrow. Now that I've seen him I'll be okay."

Gran sighs. Armstrong quiets a bit because he's pretty sure he's going to get what he wants. "All right," she finally says. "You can go home with Mrs. St. Pierre."

When I say good night to Armstrong, he winks. I grin. It took a ghost and a heart attack, not to mention beating me at crib, but I think he's finally starting to like me.

Gran, Mrs. St. Pierre and I eat dinner together in the hospital cafeteria, and then Mrs. St. Pierre and I head out to the car. I feel a bit floaty going home, disembodied by events. All flood, all the time, then this. Finally we're back in Ste. Agathe and I thank Mrs. St. Pierre. Once she's gone, I turn on all the lights in the house. I thought it would be cool to have the place to myself but it's not so much. It's just really, really quiet. I turn on the TV.

The Department of Highways and the engineering experts are all in shock about Richardson's little bombshell. They think he's right; that the current dike, which was only built to withstand a once-in-150-years flood, is too short. They have to make it longer, about forty kilometres longer, and they have to do it fast. So today they got a little truck that has a GPS in it to drive the route and they figured out where and how high the new dike extension has to be. The engineers put their heads together and figured out that if everybody works really hard, it can be ready in two months. Like that's gonna work. Alf Warkentin says we have seventy-two hours.

I'm too tired to watch any more. I write an email to Mom and Dad to tell them what's happening then crawl into bed. At first I can't sleep. I keep thinking about the papery feel of Armstrong's hand and the smell of the hospital and the look on Gran's face, but my muscles are tired…and my body feels so heavy…and I'm sinking….

The noise comes in the middle of the night. But I can't wake up. It's like I hear it, and my brain is saying "Wake up, wake up, you idiot!" but I can't drag my eyelids up. I'm not sure if I'm in a dream or if this is for real, all I know is I'm paralyzed. So heavy. I hear it again and I struggle to open my eyes. Just a crack, I manage a crack and through that crack I see a figure. I'm sure of it; there's somebody in my room. I have to wake up, I have to, and I force my head to clear and then sit up. There's nobody there. Talk about freaking myself out. First night alone in that creaky old house and look at me. I wouldn't even tell you because it makes me look like an idiot except for what happens next.

I can't sleep now because I've gone from paralyzed to high alert so I get up and go downstairs to the kitchen. And yeah, I check every room along the way. I know I was dreaming and all, but still. In the kitchen I pour a glass of milk and raid Gran's cookie jar. A couple of peanut butter cookies later there's a knock at the door. I look at the clock and it's three in the morning. There shouldn't be a knock at the door. Then I think about Armstrong and know I've got to answer it. *No, numskull, Gran would have used the phone.* I don't listen to that little voice and open the door anyway.

It's Peter. I just stand there in shock.

"How is he?"

I don't know what to say. I'm too busy checking for signs of ghostliness. I mean, what do you say to a ghost? He was way easier to talk to when I thought he was real. So I just stand there.

"HOW IS HE? It's important, Finn!"

I feel like I should reach out and see if my hand goes right through him. But that's so Hollywood. I've already touched him. I mean, he pulled me off the river and my hand didn't go through his.

"FINN!!"

"Keep your pants on. He's going to be okay. The doctor says so, and Armstrong's already complaining, so I'd say he's pretty much back to normal."

Peter sagged. "I was so worried."

"Why?"

"We're friends, I told you."

"Yeah, but rumour has it you're like a ghost or something."

Peter shakes his head in exasperation. "Or *something* would be closer. I'm here to help you, Finn. Don't you know that by now?"

"Excuse me if I get a little freaked out when I talk to a ghost *or something*."

"I take it Armstrong didn't tell you about me gently."

"You could say that."

"I'm sorry Finn, but I didn't ask for this either."

"Yeah, well. I guess not. I'll tell him you asked after him." This is so awkward. Peter nods, then turns to go down the porch steps.

"Hey," I call after him. He turns. "You weren't in my bedroom earlier, were you?"

"No, Finn. I wouldn't do that to you. That's why I knocked."

I watch him until he's out of sight.

Waking up without the sound of Gran in the kitchen makes the house feel unloved – makes me feel unloved. I know it's silly, but the quiet is so empty. It leaves room for thinking and I don't want to think about last night. I call the hospital, and the nurse says Armstrong is doing fine and that he's driving them crazy. Excellent. I tell her I'll call back at lunch and the nurse says maybe he'll be awake and can talk to me then.

When the bus drops me off at the high school, it's obvious everybody knows about Armstrong. A tonne of people come over to ask about him. Nobody's saying mean things now.

I get permission to stay at the school to fill bags for transport because I want to stay close to a phone. I left a message with the nurse for Gran to call the school if anything happens, but there aren't any calls.

When we break for lunch everybody troops into the gym, like always, to watch the TV that the principal has set up for the news. We're all addicted even though listening to the news is like riding a roller coaster. Good stories, bad stories, panic, relief, the crest goes up, the crest goes down – we can't stop listening.

So many times you hear a flood story and you think that there can't be anything crazier, and then right away something crazier comes along. Today I hear that the levees protecting this little American town called Drayton, just below the border, started to leak. They needed more clay to plug the leaks, but there was no more clay. So the mayor tells them to dig up the town's only airplane runway and use the clay to reinforce the levees. Unbelievable.

Also, today a farmer noticed that the Morris River is running backwards. Ned was way ahead of the game.

The province declares a state of emergency and seventeen thousand more people are ordered out of their homes for safety. The farmers don't want to go because they have to maintain their dikes. You can't just build it and leave it. You have to keep watching for leaks. Even I know that.

The new dike extension is being called the Brunkild Z-dike because the route it must follow in order to stick to the highest ground zigs and zags its way across the valley to the village of Brunkild. Even so, it has to be at least two and a half metres high. Two-and-a-half metres times forty kilometres equals twenty million sandbags, give or take. I'm going to check with Hazel, because I just don't think this is going to work.

Two more people die today. One of them was a fourteen-year-old boy. Just a year older than me.

There are thousands of reporters in Manitoba now, so many you could say they are flooding the airwaves – ha ha. Peter Mansbridge, the anchor on CBC television, has just arrived to cover the flood and everybody's saying that his being here officially makes this a disaster. Now we can panic. As far as I'm concerned, the media is just confusing things. The government says, "Don't worry, everything's under control" and the TV says, "OMG, what a disaster!" It's hard to know who's right. And for some reason, the reporters are all looking for stories about things that go wrong. They should talk about this instead. Clara kissed me. I know it was because of Armstrong, but still.

I call the hospital again and get to talk to both Armstrong and Gran. He's doing great and is full of instructions on what I have to do at our place, especially what to look for as I check the section of dike that's close to the house. One little heart attack and I'm no longer fallout but his main guy. Gran has other ideas. She talked to Aaron's mother and the two of them have arranged for me to go and stay with Aaron until Gran comes home. I hear some spluttering in the background, but I can tell from Gran's tone that she's going to win this one. I'm torn. I haven't told Armstrong about Peter's visit yet and there's no way I'm telling Gran he was at the house. But I'm not looking forward to a repeat visit. Staying with Aaron would be great, but what about the dikes? Armstrong's right, somebody has to be here. I kind of feel like I should have a say, I mean, if I'm grown-up enough to be responsible for a dike, you'd think I should be able to decide where I sleep.

But apparently not. I'm going to Aaron's, so I promise Armstrong that I'll hitch a ride with somebody every day to come back and check the dike. He stops spluttering and I get back to work.

Mrs. Taylor is fantastic. She picks me and Aaron up at the school then drives straight to Gran's to help me check the dike.

I give Mrs. Taylor my house key and she checks inside. Aaron and I head over to the dike. As we pass the barn I almost tell him, almost show him the catfish, but I don't. When we get close to the clump of trees at the river, I climb over the dike and check the riverbank. No Peter. When I get back up, Aaron is waving a huge magic marker in my face.

"What?"

"I think you should mark your territory," he says with a grin. "Like a dog does."

"Dogs don't use magic markers," I say.

"Yeah, but my mom's watching, dummy," says Aaron. "Mark your territory."

So I take the marker and write my name in big letters across the plastic that's covering the dike. FINN ARMSTRONG. Then I grin at Aaron and write AARON TAYLOR. Then I write FLOOD-FIGHTERS! Aaron grins up at me.

Back at his place we have burgers and fries then watch a movie. Later, Aaron's dad helps him shower and get ready for bed while I play a video game and try not to think about what they're doing. That's sure something I didn't think about, having to let somebody carry you and wash you and who knows what else, even if it is your dad. His mom puts a blow up mattress beside Aaron's bed and fixes it up with sheets and a blanket. Aaron likes to sleep in absolute, total darkness. I like that too. It lets us talk.

"I'm really sorry about your legs."

"Yeah. Whatever."

"Not whatever! It's really a bummer."

I can hear him shift the covers. "No, I mean it, man.

Whatever. When it first happened I was totally pissed. It wasn't my fault, I wasn't doing anything stupid, so why me? I thought my life was over. But after awhile I understood that only that life was over, the one with legs that worked. The one I have now isn't less, just different. And then I wasn't so mad any more. I started to think of all the things I was going to do now that I wouldn't have done with legs. You know how people say "go with the flow"? The flow's taking me to a different place, but I'm still going somewhere."

I think about this for a minute. "I think I know what you mean. This isn't the same at all, but I kind of felt that way when my parents told me I had to come here. I was supposed to go to Egypt and I was really mad. But now I'm glad I came."

"Yeah," says Aaron. "That's it all right."

The quiet that comes after isn't empty.

CHAPTER 10

Clara

The Red River crosses the border and crests at Emerson. It's now 28 kilometres wide and officially the biggest river in North America, even bigger than the Mississippi. Thanks to the soldiers, Emerson's dikes hold, but there's a new problem: wind. It's blowing the floodwaters out across the valley and creating waves that are a metre high – dike-destroying waves. Morris is the next town upriver and it's under attack. Flood Stop #4.

More bags, more trucks. It's endless. I think I'm getting a six-pack, an Armstrong first. Mrs. Taylor takes me to check our dike after work and everything's okay. No water, no Peter. I call the hospital to check on Armstrong and Gran says she'll be home tomorrow. They're keeping Armstrong in Winnipeg, more because of the uncertainty around the flood than the heart attack, which is making him cross and Gran relieved. Then it's back to Aaron's for pizza with the whole gang. I'm still amazed that a disaster can feel so much like a party. Except at a party we'd watch a video instead of the news. It turns out to be way more exciting than some dumb Hollywood movie.

Today, every piece of digging equipment from every construction site and every farm for a hundred kilometres was moved to the Brunkild Dike. Watching four hundred diggers in action all at the same time is really something. We are glued to the TV. The crews have to work all night so helicopters hover overhead, dropping flares attached to baby parachutes so the volunteers can see. It's wild, and so is the weather: cold, wet and windy.

After the news we just mellow out. Aaron and I talk about places in the world we want to visit. Jane and Roy are mapping the flood on a map, colouring all the places that are under water with blue highlighter. The blue parts are growing and growing and getting closer and closer to us. I find out that Jane has five brothers. No wonder she's so easygoing. And Roy is actually a super-promising hockey player, even though he's always putting down his team. Hazel's running calculations to figure out how many sandbags the Flood Club has filled. Before the Flood Club, she was president of the Latin Club. I didn't even know there was one. Clara's an only child, and she's really close to her mom. Her dad is dead. She's really quiet tonight.

Next morning, Mrs. Taylor drops us off at the school parking lot. Now that Armstrong is for sure doing okay, and I don't have to be around for any emergency phone calls, I ask to be sent out to help build dikes. I'm good at it. I love to see the walls of white bags grow around somebody's life and know that I'm helping them protect what they love the most. At night on the news we get to see our work from the air as the news helicopters fly overhead and film all these white-ringed islands sticking up out of the water. Baby Noah's arks, that's what they look like. Trouble is, about a quarter of those arks are sinking. I thought we were safe, but not all of the dikes are holding. We have to do better.

Clara asks to be assigned to dike-building too, so we're on the same bus. We're heading south today, toward the oncoming water to help farmers plug leaks. It's the last chance to try to help them. Usually the high-school students are kept out of the danger zone, but the closer the water comes the fewer safe zones are left.

"You're really quiet, Clara. What's the matter?"

She doesn't say anything. I just wait.

Finally, "It's my sisters. I'm really worried about them. They live outside of Morris, and I've been calling them every day. I couldn't get through yesterday. My dad is such a dork, I'm sure if he even bothered to build a dike around his house it would fall apart. What if something's happened to the twins?"

Whoa. There are tears in her eyes. This is for real, except for the minor point that she's not supposed to have a dad or any sisters, let alone twins. "Come again?"

So she tells me her story, her *real* story. When Bert, her dad, decided to leave her mom and her, it wasn't because there was another woman or anything. He just said he'd rather be alone than have to live with them. Talk about harsh. Her mom felt like she was less than nothing, so she moved to Easthaven and made up this story that he'd died, so people wouldn't think she was a complete loser.

"I was okay with that because I felt the same way. I was only six, but I heard him say he couldn't stand being with us and even a six-year-old understands that. But a year ago I started wondering about him. I mean, Mom and I are doing okay, better than okay, and I'm not afraid that we're losers any more. He's the one who's a loser. We have friends, so obviously some people can stand to be with us."

I squeeze her hand. I sure can. She gives me a sad little smile.

"Maybe his life was a mess because he left us. It's cruel, but I almost wished that it was. So I looked him up and found out that he lived in Morris and he'd married again and had twin daughters, three years old. That changed everything for me. I had sisters! Only half-sisters, but I always hated being an only child. So one Saturday I told Mom I was going to Jane's, but instead, I took the bus to Morris. I went to their house and pretended to sell magazine subscriptions for school. Lame, but it was all I could think of and the band really was selling subscriptions."

"Finn, she was so nice. I wanted to hate her because she stole my mom's life, but she was just like my mom. And while we were talking the twins came to the door and they looked just like I did when I was little."

"That must have freaked you out," I say.

"I started bawling. It was so embarrassing. And then I told her who I was. And it turns out that all the time we were pretending that Dad was dead he was telling his new wife how great Mom and I were. It made no sense, but then he's a total jerk."

"Anyway, since then I've kept in touch with her and the twins. My mom doesn't know and my dad doesn't know. Nobody does except you. I've been so worried about them but up until two days ago Barb, that's his new wife, said they were fine. Everything was okay. But I don't think it is any more. Finn, can you help me find them?"

"Morris coming up! Get ready!"

I look out the window. Morris is being evacuated. On the opposite side of the highway is a long line of cars, trucks and campers filled with worried-looking people heading north toward the city. It's the only way they can go. The Red River is herding them from behind. All of us have water up to our axles and it feels like we're in the middle of an ocean.

"Maybe they're driving out, and that's why you can't reach them," I say quietly to Clara.

She just shakes her head. "Dad would never be that smart."

Our bus drives through the ring dike. Once everybody's out, the last remaining soldiers will put sandbags over the road to plug the last hole in the dike and leave Morris to its fate. Inside the dike, it's dry. Store clerks are emptying the stuff on their shelves into moving trucks. Families are stuffing chairs and rugs and framed pictures into cars and trucks. It feels organized, though, all except for the herd of white-tailed deer that are caught inside the dike and are wandering around downtown. Lucky for them. When the bus stops I grab Clara's hand. Morris is full of soldiers. With soldiers, all you have to do is look around and it's pretty easy to see who's in charge. That's the guy I go for.

"There's a problem," I say. "Clara knows of a family that probably didn't make it out. They might be cut off. Can you help?"

"That's what we're here for," said the soldier. "Do you think you can find their place?" he asks Clara. She nods. The soldier, whose name is Bruce, takes us to a command post and points to a map that's spread out on a table. "Where do they live?"

Clara points. Then we get hustled to a Zodiac and are handed life preservers. It turns out that Bruce is with the Navy. He says he never thought he'd be posted to the prairies. I guess not. Bruce starts the motor and we're off. You know I said this flood was like a roller coaster? Right now it's more like a mechanical bull. Clara and I hang on for dear life as the boat pitches forward and back, pounding, pounding, pounding against the water that is heaving into giant whitecaps. How is it that such shallow water can make such big waves? I'm not sure if I've broken my neck or ditched my stomach. Then the ride turns into bumper cars as Bruce tries to avoid the tips of street signs and traffic lights and then, farther out, the tops of trees that are poking up through the surface. I don't know how we're going to find anything out here. As far as I can tell, everything's gone.

Bruce keeps consulting a hand-held GPS, and soon we see a roof off to the left. "That's it!" Clara tries to shout. I can only see her lips move, I can't hear a thing. Bruce slows the Zodiac and we putt-putt toward the roof. As we get close, Clara starts to cry.

Shivering on top of the roof are Bert and Barb. Sitting, one on each lap, are the twins, covered in mud and sobbing. When the boat comes close, Barb starts to cry too. "I thought we'd be out here forever," she chokes. "I thought we were going to die!"

Bruce is amazing. He talks in such a calm voice that everybody settles down. He has me go up on the roof to help hand the twins down to him because Clara's dad is so cold that he can't trust his hands. We get the twins off then I help Barb. Clara's dad shrugs off my help, but in the end, we're both in the boat. Bruce hands out life jackets. The whole operation comes off with military precision. It's impossible to talk once we get moving so we don't know what happened to them but it's pretty easy to guess. Barb is furious now that she's been rescued and Bert looks like he wants to start a fight. Whatever their plan was, it didn't work and they're blaming each other. Well, at least they're alive. They can fight later, once Clara and I are far, far away.

Except that's not going to happen for a while. Bruce is having trouble with the Zodiac. The sky has darkened even though it's still early, and the wind is really whipping up. Then the rain comes. Just what we need, more water. We're getting pounded and now it's not just waves Bruce has to deal with, but a ferocious current as well. He slows down. Then he hits the top of a road sign and the propeller nearly breaks off, at least that's what it feels like. He heads toward some grass sticking out of the water and yells, "There shouldn't be anything hard over there." Turns out the "grass" is really treetops. I can't believe the water is that deep. The sky is getting darker and darker, and Bruce is really having trouble. Being in the trees is even worse, so he heads back out into the monstrous sea of murky water. I see a huge, long hulking thing up ahead and point. Maybe it's the town? Bruce motors toward it. It isn't the town, it's a long line of railway cars just peeking out of the water. Bruce yells again, "They left them here to try to hold down the tracks."

Hold down the railway tracks? The current is strong enough to rip up railway tracks? We're getting pushed this way and that, I don't know if it's the wind or the current or both, but I don't even know what direction we're going in any more. Bruce keeps checking his GPS as if he doesn't either. All the girls are huddled together and Clara's dad is just sitting in the front of the boat, looking down at the floorboards. He's no help. I look at Bruce. I'm pretty sure he's lost.

Then all of a sudden, it's like I'm in the movies. You know that part in an action film when the music starts to build and it's all you can hear and you see the characters yell at one another while they try to save themselves but all you can hear is the music and it's cosmic because you know that in the next second they're either going to be saved or they're going to die but you don't know which and it doesn't really matter because the music lifts you up and out of the scene and you can see everything from a distance? You know what I mean?

That's what happens next. Suddenly, I'm looking at the scene from outside the boat, at least that's what it feels like, and it isn't me in the boat. It's Peter. And Peter looks straight at me where I'm hovering or flying or whatever I'm doing, and he leans over the side of the motorboat and points down at the water. And he smiles. There isn't any music, there isn't any sound at all, just silence. And then I'm back in the boat and the wind is screaming and I look over the side and I can see fish. Big fish with spiny fins sticking out of the water and tentacles all squirmy around their mouths. Big fish swimming fast and hard right alongside us. The fish start to swim east, and when I look up to see where they're going, I see the dikes of Morris. I point and Bruce smiles and sticks his useless GPS into his pocket. We're home.

There really should be music.

There are lots of helping hands to get Clara's family out of the Zodiac, and she goes off to get them hooked up with an evacuation truck. Bruce shakes my hand and then it's over. In the end I rescue, not the beautiful sidekick, but the dad she despises. So much for my special powers.

Don't worry, I know that nothing really happened in the boat. I didn't really float and I didn't really see Peter, except in my mind's eye because I'll admit it, I was scared, and that does funny things to your brain. Seeing the catfish just snapped me out it and calmed me down enough so that I could look around and figure out where we were. That's all.

Really.

After that, Clara and I are put to work filling bags and loading them on boats for the soldiers to take to the leaky spots in the dikes. No more boats for us and that's okay by me. Bag, toss, bag, toss. Just a day in the life of a floodfighter.

We stop early because everybody's got to get out of Morris. The river's due to crest and only a skeleton crew is going to stay to plug the dike. Farmers are parking their combines and tractors on one side of the road to try to keep them out of the advancing water. Clara and I don't say anything all the way home, we just look out the window. Water stretches from horizon to horizon. The only thing I can see, other than water, are the lonely ringed farmhouses dotting the surface. Today I saw what happens when the dikes don't hold, and it scares me. This isn't fun any more. I reach over and take Clara's hand and she lets me.

Back at the school, I see Gran's smiling face waiting for me. Just looking at her makes me think of cookies and it's the happiest thought I've had all day.

"How's Armstrong?" I ask.

"Driving the nurses crazy," she smiles.

That means he feels good. I punch the air in a cheer. "All right, Armstrong!"

Gran, Clara and I head over to the rest of the gang hanging around Mrs. Taylor's car. We compare notes on the day, and all I say is that Clara and I helped rescue a stranded family. Gran looks horrified, Roy looks jealous and Aaron can tell there's more to it. But we leave the story there. I get my stuff out of Aaron's car. As Gran and I turn to go to our car, I quietly ask Clara if she's okay. She says yes, but we both know she's lying. I don't know what to do to help her.

Gran's obviously glad to be home because today's cookie is double-reverse chocolate with peanut-butter chips. She makes dinner while I shower, then we sit down to watch Plugged In. The RCMP wants to know what roads to close. The railroads want to know how long they can schedule trains through the valley. Only Peter can answer those questions. More interesting is the news about the Brunkild dike. It's amazing, and the people building it are even more amazing. Private contractors, the government and the military are all working together. Farmers whose land is going to be cut in half by the dike, half flooded and half saved, don't bother arguing about it, they just lend their equipment to help dig up their fields. Dozens of backhoes are grabbing earth and piling it high. Bulldozers are pounding it down. Huge trucks full of limestone from quarries north of the city bump along the top of the emerging dike, adding fill. Cranes drop giant one-and-a-half tonne sandbags into place. There are lots of men whose only job is to talk into walkie-talkies to prevent all the machines from running into each other. There's video of hundreds of soldiers and volunteers trying to staple down kilometres of plastic wrap and snow fencing over the parts that are finished, their hair and clothing practically blowing off their bodies in the strong wind. The man in charge of getting the dike built is Kuryk. If it works, he's going to be a hero. The only lucky thing is that the wind is blowing from the north, blowing the water away from the dike, south toward Morris. If it weren't for that, there's no way it would be finished in time. But poor Morris.

Today a lot of us get sent to Grande Pointe. It's a suburb of Winnipeg and it has a foot of water everywhere. The flood hasn't reached Grande Pointe yet, so no one can figure out where the water is coming from. Nobody likes surprises like this one. When we get there, all of us except Aaron (bag-tosser extraordinaire) are sent to the elementary school. There aren't any kids, but the teachers are trying to pack up their classrooms and get the expensive stuff, like computers, out of harm's way. Like I said, nobody likes surprises and Grande Pointe wasn't supposed to flood.

Clara looks better this morning. She gave me a hug first thing and real quiet, said that she told her mother about Barb and the twins. Wow, I bet the two of them had a night of it.

"Yeah, we talked until really late. But I feel so much better now. Before, I sort of felt like I was betraying Mom. But she says she wants to meet Barb and the twins. Wouldn't that be great?"

I think back to the way Barb and Bert were treating each other yesterday. It sure was different from the way my parents treat each other, or Aaron's parents. "Maybe your mom and Barb can start their own Survivors of Bert Support Group?"

Clara looks shocked for a second then bursts out laughing. We both get back to packing computers and loading them onto trucks for safekeeping. By the time we're done, there's water lapping at the tires.

At dinner that night, Armstrong calls. He sounds great. He and Gran talk for a while and then I get the phone.

"Finn, you need to walk our dike. Check the plastic, make sure it hasn't blown away anywhere. If it's torn, there's more plastic in the shed by the river. Overlap the torn place and spike it down. Extra spikes are in the shed as well. And most important, check for leaks."

"Armstrong, there's no water around the dikes. There can't be any leaks, at least not yet."

"Check anyway. Check with your eyes, but especially with your ears. You'll hear a leak before you see it. And the sump pump in the basement, you know how to work it?"

"Yeah. You showed me."

"If the electricity goes it will switch to battery power. If the battery goes dead the pump will overflow. You can't let that happen. There's an extra battery in the green cupboard in the basement. Make sure you watch the pump and switch to a new battery if you have to. It's really important, Finn. If the pump overflows, the basement will flood."

"Got it: extra battery, green cupboard."

I can hear the worry in his voice. I know he wants to be here, but I'm glad he's not. I hate to think of him walking the dike in the dark, especially since I'm here. I mean, he's ninety-four! I know how to do it.

"One more thing, Finn. Your Gran is going to get some of the men from the village to move our furniture upstairs. We've never had to do that before so it's going to upset her. Your job is to stick with her, make her feel better, while they do the moving. Agreed?"

"But why, Armstrong? Ste. Agathe isn't going to flood!"

"It *probably* won't. But is *probably* a good enough reason for your Gran to lose her flowered chair?"

"Okaaaay, Armstrong, okay." I'm pretty skeptical, but of course I'll help Gran. I mean, duh. Armstrong's just full of orders today. "Get everything packed up as if you're going to evacuate, just as a precaution. Then if you have to go, you're ready. Got it?" Now I see why the nurses are getting ticked off with him.

That night we hear that the dikes around Morris hold. Yippee!

CHAPTER 11

The Middle

Next day Gran's got a whole posse of fellows from the village and it feels like moving day. Thank goodness our house has a second storey. Everything except the piano gets moved upstairs, and they even prop the piano up on a bunch of paint cans from the shed so it's a little higher, anyway. I tell the guys to put Gran's flowered chair in her bedroom and make sure there's nothing stashed on top of it so it's still sit-able. The kitchen table is in Armstrong's bedroom so it looks like that's where we'll be eating from now on. Talk about weird. I try to help Gran, but she's doing fine with all this, better than me. I tell you, it's freakin' me out.

"Hey, Mrs. Armstrong, what about the barn? Anything in there that needs lifting?" calls out one of the guys.

Whoa. I look at Gran real quick and she gives me a little shake of her head. "No, it's empty, fellows, but thank you."

Once they're gone I ask, "What about the channel cats?"

Gran sighs. "What about them? For one thing, most of the shelves are pretty high, so they'll probably be all right. But even if they're not, don't you think people are going to ask questions if they know Armstrong's got a couple of hundred wooden catfish in his barn? Do you want to be the one to answer those questions?"

No way.

It's the sirens that wake me. I roll over to look at the clock and it's only five in the morning. What the heck? I put the covers over my head and try to go back to sleep, but then Gran's in my room, shaking me.

"No," I groan. "It's too early. Let me sleep!"

"Finn, get up," she says urgently. "The soldiers are here. We have to evacuate. We have to leave *now*."

That gets me going, all right. I rush to the window, but there's no water. The river's high, but it hasn't spilled over its banks. "It's okay, Gran, we've got time." I throw on some clothes and start moving. The sirens wail on and on. "Heard you already," I mumble. We're all ready, thanks to Armstrong, but it still feels like a shock. Gran drives the truck around and backs it close to the front door. Our boxes are there and waiting, so I load them into the back of the pickup. One soldier helps me load while another hands Gran a checklist.

"This will help you evacuate smoothly, ma'am." Gran and I take a look at the list:

1. Register with the Winnipeg police, including both your present and future address.
2. Turn the furnace off.
3. Turn the water supply off.
4. Call the gas company to shut off the gas supply.

5. Leave electricity on if you have a working sump pump.
6. Empty food from refrigerator and freezer. Take it with you to avoid possible spoilage in the event of power outages.
7. Place houseplants in a bathtub with a few inches of water.
8. Arrange for household pets to either accompany you or be boarded out.
9. Lock your door.

Done, done and done. Once everything is ready to go, Gran gets into the truck. "Hop in," she says. I walk around to her window.

"Gran, I'm not going."

"Yes, you are, young man."

"I need to stay and look after the dike, and the pump. Armstrong is counting on me."

"Not on your life, Finlay Gordon Armstrong! I don't care about the dike or the basement. I care about you. And if the government thinks we're in danger, we're going. Full stop."

I argue.

Gran argues back.

"What if you have to be rescued? What if other people have to put their lives at risk because you were stupid? Think about that family you rescued and about what could have happened to all of you because they chose not to leave when they should have. Haven't you learned *anything* in these last few weeks?"

"I've learned that it's all about the dikes. The dikes, Gran! And look, the water is nowhere close. I'm not saying I shouldn't evacuate ever, just not yet."

A couple of the soldiers come over to the truck. "Is there a problem, ma'am?" asks one of them.

Gran is all spluttery as she tells the soldier how foolish I want to be. The soldier looks at my red shirt. "Is it just the two of you here?"

"I know how to check the dike," I insist.

"Ma'am, I'd highly recommend you go. Son, do you know the rules about refusing an evacuation order?"

"Yes. I can only stay if I have a ring dike, three weeks worth of food, communication and an escape route. Check, check and check."

"What's your escape route?"

"My friend Aaron's house, over in Easthaven. The water gets even close to the top of the dikes and I'm outta here." I look the soldier in the eye. "I was helping in Morris. I know what can happen if you wait too long."

The soldier nods. "You sound pretty organized, but you should listen to your grandmother. Listen, a skeleton crew is staying on here in Ste. Agathe to watch the dikes. There will be some local people who know the area and some soldiers to help them. You don't have to be here. It makes no sense to wait until the last minute, because that's when you're going to get into trouble."

"But…"

"But nothing, young man," says Gran firmly. "There are lives at stake here, Finn, and nobody knows for sure what the flood will do. It only makes sense to err on the side of caution."

I get that what the dikes are trying to protect is only stuff. But that's not what this is about. It's about not letting the river win. Gran doesn't get it.

"Okay?" she asks.

"No!" But I go get my bag because it's not like I ever get to decide anything for myself. I go downstairs, throw it in the back of the truck and head for the passenger door. Then I look up at the barn.

"Wait a minute," I tell Gran. I go back into the kitchen and grab Armstrong's key ring. I take it to the barn, unlock the padlock and slide the chains through the door handles. I have to open the doors wide to get enough light, but it helps that I know where to look. I take my channel cat off the shelf that Armstrong has marked 1997. I take another look at all those shadowy catfish and think about what this particular school of fish means. Somehow I have to get all this to start making sense in my head, but I honestly don't know if I can. Not right now, anyway. I close the barn doors, replace the padlock and walk back to the truck. I wrap my catfish in a sweatshirt and stick it in the top of my bag. Now I'm ready.

Mrs. Taylor is great as always. She gets Gran settled in their guest room and I'm back on the mattress in Aaron's room. The day is pretty much gone, so Aaron and I decide to watch Plugged In. Watching the Z-Dike get longer and taller is totally awesome. It's so big that now they're calling it the Brunkild Bunker. I could watch for hours.

"Hey, Aaron, wouldn't it be cool to work on that dike?"

Aaron looks thoughtful for a minute. "Nope, I wouldn't want to be there."

"Why? Because of your wheelchair?"

"No, but could you see me doing wheelies around those big trucks? It'd be bumper cars with the big guys!" We have a laugh.

"Nah." he says. "There's too much pressure on those guys.

If they don't finish it in time or if it fails, the whole city goes. If I were one of those guys, I'd be having a heart attack right about now."

I think about that for a while until I get what Aaron's saying.

"You don't think it's going to work, do you?"

Aaron looks at me. "Nope."

Next day the whole Flood Club gets bused into Winnipeg. We've done all we can do for the farmers so the city's all that's left. I really want to go because of what Aaron said, about how he thinks the Bunker isn't going to hold. That's the huge worry now. Anyway, we get bused to this place called Scotia Street. The military is already here and there are lots of volunteers too, even some other high schools. Everybody's heard of us because we were the first high school to get going, so as soon as they see our red shirts they cheer. All right! Right away they're on us to do a gumboot dance and of course we go for it. Us farm folks have to show the city kids how it's done. The other kids join in and the soldiers clap and then it's all hands on deck. There's work to be done.

The stories you hear from the city sandbag brigades are different from the ones we're used to hearing. A lot of the volunteers are office workers. Their bosses let them off work to help. Some people who already have their homes sandbagged have spray-painted messages on the plastic covering the dikes. Hey, just like Aaron and me. The messages say stuff like "We will win!" and "No man is an island." Yep, ya got that right. There are people helping from all over the country. The airlines are offering cheap flights to anybody who wants to fly to

Winnipeg to help, and that's not all they're doing. I heard this one story about a flight attendant who had a layover in Chicago. There's a little plug that you can use to screw into your sewer line and it stops sewage water from backing up into your basement so of course everybody wants one, but every single hardware store in all of Canada is sold out. So this flight attendant is in Chicago and spends the day buying up all the sewer plugs in the whole city. She flies back to Winnipeg with 273 plugs in her carry-on luggage. Very cool.

It's even more like a war zone in the city. There are so many army vehicles and soldiers, and even big, heavy military helicopters flying overhead that it feels scarier than in the country. And there's so much worry. Everything that's happening here is more intense, somehow, and the people are more stressed. Even the sandbag brigades are bigger and faster. So when the Flood Club breaks into a song (because that's just what we do), the other baggers are shocked. But then they join in and it's like a mass choir, if you can imagine a choir that's sweaty and covered in mud. You should see the expressions on the homeowners' faces when they look out their window and see our sandbag brigade lining up in front of their house to help save it. We don't know them and they don't know us, but it doesn't matter. And when their house is done, they bring out donuts and coffee, and sometimes they cry. There are notes tacked to trees all over the city that say "Thank you, volunteers." Everybody's smiling. Nobody's complaining. I can't tell you how proud I feel to be part of this. Dad should really be studying the Red River people. We're special.

At noon they take us to the St. Vital Arena for lunch. It's

turned into an evacuation centre for people who have no place else to go. Some of the people who are here have already lost their homes and they just sit on cots, staring out into space, probably wondering what they're going to do next. Others talk about how hard it was to leave their houses, not knowing if they'd ever see them again. Yeah, I get that. And there's one old guy handing out donated stuffed animals to all the little kids that come in. He's real smiley and happy, but somebody told me he just heard that his dike failed and his house is flooded. You'd never know it by looking at him.

I feel overwhelmed by the end of the day, not by the bagging, because that's second nature now, but by all the stories and all the worry. When the six of us get back into the handicapped bus (we ride with Aaron now), Jane says it all.

"Epic."

Oh, yeah.

Next day we're stuck at home. The water's too close now, the highways are either flooded or about to be, and Winnipeg's an island. We all are. There's nothing to do but watch the water rise around us. We're glued to the Plugged In channel on TV. We watch the water move north, spreading out in all directions as it goes. The news cameras are on helicopters so we get a bird's eye view of the Red Sea, which is the new name for the Red River. It's thirty-eight kilometres wide now, dotted with white-ringed islands. The helicopters fly over the Brunkild Dike as it steadily grows on its zigzag route to the west, ready to hold back the ocean of water. The experts reckon that the water is just three kilometres away from it. Roy and Jane are on their second set of blue highlighters, so much of their map is covered in water now. In another few days it will be over, one way or another.

That night I can't sleep.

"Aaron, are you awake?"

"Yeah."

I take a deep breath. "Do you believe in ghosts?"

"Whaddya mean, ghosts?"

"I mean, do you think that somebody who's dead can come back and look like a normal person and talk like a normal person, but know stuff about the future that nobody else can know?"

He takes a long time answering, but at least he doesn't laugh.

"Maybe," he says carefully. "Do you?"

"Maybe," I say back just as carefully.

A while goes by then Aaron says, "Why?"

Here goes. I'm so glad of the dark. "Because I think I met one."

Another silence, then, "That's intense."

"Yeah," I admit. "I'm a little freaked out."

So then I tell him about Peter, about Armstrong, about the wooden catfish and what Gran said. There's another long silence. Then, "Can I see it?"

Aaron turns the light back on. I reach into my bag and unwrap the catfish from my sweatshirt. By the light of Aaron's lamp, it looks just as beautiful as it did when Peter gave it to me. Aaron takes it and slowly rubs his index finger along the grain. He feels the carved fins, the huge mouth and the barb-like tentacles.

"And you say there are hundreds of these in Armstrong's barn?"

I nod my head.

"Geez, Finn."

"Yeah."

CHAPTER 12

The End

May 1997

Next day the wind changes direction from north to west. The Brunkild Bunker is just about finished but if the wind starts blowing from the south the water will get pushed right into it and it may not hold. The Red Sea is so big that if the wind changes, the wave action will be ferocious. The dike needs a breakwater to protect it. The experts put their heads together again and come up with a plan. We all watch on TV as huge cranes dump dozens and dozens of junkyard cars and old school buses in a line in front of the dike. This is awesome.

It's two-thirty in the morning, and I wake up because I think I hear something. I keep hearing it, but I can't figure out what it is, so I get up and go to the back door. Maybe I can hear better outside. I pass the kitchen and I see Mrs. Taylor and Gran sitting there. Mrs. Taylor is holding Gran's hand and Gran is crying.

"Is it Armstrong?" I demand.

Mrs. Taylor shakes her head. Gran looks up at me.

"Listen, Finn."

I listen. Now I can hear that it's church bells ringing in the distance, that's what the sound is. I look at Gran, feeling a bit confused, and she looks...she looks stricken.

"The Ste. Agathe church bells, that's the signal," she whispers. "The signal that our dikes have been breached."

Mrs. Taylor makes tea. There's nothing we can do except wait for somebody to call and tell us what happened. Tell us if everybody who stayed behind to mind the dikes got out. Tell us how much water came in. Tell us what we lost. Tell us what went wrong. Tell us why.

We don't hear anything until morning. It's a very long night. That's because the floodwatchers in Ste. Agathe didn't get out — not for hours and hours, not until dawn. They were trapped, but finally we hear the whole story.

Last night, the river was high, but the east side of the dike was holding it back. The water was half a metre below the top of the dike. No worries. The worst problem was that west wind, which had blown up into a real gale. I bet it was miserable.

But the water didn't come from the river. No sirree. The water came from the back, from the west side of the village. I'll bet the flood watchers were thinking, "You're kidding me right?" You've got a village with a river running along the east side and the floodwater comes from the west, from the open prairie? Impossible. They say one of the floodwatchers on the south end of Main Street saw it first. He called it in on his walkie-talkie.

"Water's building up where the tracks go through."

Then somebody says, "Do you hear that?"

"It sounds like rapids."

"It's coming. Let's hightail it out of here."

"Water's pouring in through the tracks."

"It's a wall of water!"

Then the final call: "Get out! Get out!"

The dike didn't fail. We built it well and it held. Trouble is, there's a place where the railway tracks go through the dike. The railway tracks are on a raised embankment so it forms a natural dike. Our sandbags went right up to the railway embankment. But last night, the embankment wasn't high enough. A wall of water came up and over it with a great whoosh. The water gushed over the tracks and ran down Main Street, spreading in all directions. Then another wall of water came over.

They say all the floodwatchers were running down Main Street when there was *another* whoosh of water. They were already ankle-deep. One of the guys ran to the church and started ringing the bells. Then all the floodwatchers met at the assembly point – the water was still rising. Everybody hopped into the escape truck, but by now the water was up to the head-lights and the truck couldn't move. One of the soldiers radioed for help and, after a while, an armoured personnel carrier, one of those things that can be a truck or a boat, came sailing into Ste. Agathe and picked everybody up. They were on the boat for a long, long time because there was no dry land to put them down on. Talk about feeling like Noah.

They say there are almost two meters of water in the village. So much for the piano. Gran calls Armstrong and they talk for a long time, but I don't want to talk to anybody. I feel – cheated. I worked so hard, we all did, and for what? The river tricked us.

There are quite a few people from the village staying with friends and family in Easthaven like us, and before long everybody from Ste. Agathe has made their way to the local coffee shop. Everybody passes on what they've heard, but it all just makes the story more confusing because nobody actually knows anything for sure. The one big question – how much did we lose? – can't be answered until the military lets us go back home, and that won't be for days. Go home? That's if we still have one.

I can't stand all the maybe, maybe, maybe talk so I head back to Aaron's and the rest of the gang follows. No one knows what to say to me, I can tell. It's like somebody died. Finally Roy decides to get mad on my behalf.

"It's just not fair! I mean, you helped start the Flood Club! You helped saved tonnes of other people's properties. Man, it just shouldn't be you, that's all I'm sayin' here."

Everybody agrees, Roy's got this whole cheering section for his theory, and sure, it would be great if the flood recognized hard work and flowed around the properties of the people who deserved to stay dry. But it didn't. What a colossally stupid notion.

"Don't be an idiot!" I shout. Then I get up and leave. Even that's hard to do because I don't have my own room to go to and I just have to hope that Aaron's smart enough to leave me alone. If he's not, I'm going to hit him. And part of me is saying *You don't want to do that because he's somebody you just trusted with your deepest secret.* The other part of me is saying *Stuff it! Why can't they just leave me alone?*

I can hear them out in the living room. It's a nasty feeling when you know your friends are talking about you. That doesn't help my mood one bit. I try to sleep so I can shut down for a while – I'm too revved up. I want to throw something, but I'm really not that kind of person. I don't do stuff like that. And knowing that I'm being selfish because I really should be helping my Gran, who's lost way more than I have, makes me feel even worse.

There's a knock on the bedroom door.

"WHAT?"

"Can I come in?" It's Clara.

"NO."

"Thanks," she says as she comes in and sits on Aaron's bed. I just glare at her. "We want to come to your party."

"What are you talking about?"

"This pity party you're having right now. We want to come. We've even got snacks."

Okay, so I have to laugh. "Snacks?"

"Yeah, special pity party snacks. So come on."

"No, thanks."

"Wrong answer." With that, she tries to pull me up off my mattress. When that doesn't work, she kicks me. She actually kicks me.

"Hey!"

"I'm not leaving until you get up," she says. And she looks like she means it. So what choice does a guy have?

I let her pull me into the kitchen. There are a few tentative smiles, but everybody's wary.

"You said there were snacks." It's all I can think to say.

Jane and Hazel jump up. Aaron directs and they get bowls,

spoons and ice cream. I just watch. Jane scoops ice cream into the bowls then mashes each scoop with a spoon, making it look disgusting. Clara sprinkles Smarties on top of the ice cream. She hands one bowl to me. Then Hazel hands me a squirt bottle of chocolate sauce.

"That ice cream," says Clara, "is the prairie. Those Smarties are ring dikes. The chocolate sauce is disgustingly mucky, dirty Red River water. You are now officially in charge of flooding, so you may go ahead and flood whatever ring dike you please."

Oh, come on.

"Go ahead," says Hazel. "Pick a dike to drown."

"Nah," says Roy. "Drown 'em all!"

This is too ridiculous. Smartie ring dikes? Roy grabs the squirt bottle out of my hands and floods one of my Smarties.

"Hey, you said I was in charge!" I grab the bottle and flood all his Smarties. He grabs it back and we fight over it. Unfortunately Aaron's face is in the way and ends up covered in chocolate.

I'm not going to tell you the rest of this part of the story. I think you can guess. The cleanup, as Jane says, was epic.

It's hard to watch Plugged In any more because for Gran and I, the flood is over. Who knew that we were going to be Flood Stop #5? The worst has already happened. I try to worry for all the people in Winnipeg who are waiting for what they call C-Day, or Crest Day, but I can't, especially since tonight the news is good for a change. The height of the crest is revised downwards and in Morris the water level has gone down a couple of centimetres. That means the end of the flood is coming. Just the same, I watch with everybody else because there's nothing else to do. We can't go home.

The water has reached the Brunkild Dike. It holds. But then the wind shifts to the south and we're back to the worst case scenario. An evacuation order goes out for ten thousand more people who live on the other side of the dike, just in case. It feels like the whole valley is holding its breath.

Overnight the water rises one-and-a-half metres against the Bunker. By six a.m. it's within fifteen centimetres of the top, and the wind is gale force. Large waves topped with whitecaps blow across the expanse of the Red Sea with nothing to stop them between the American border and Brunkild. They pound the dike and the south side starts to erode, in spite of all the trashed cars and school buses. Crews frantically race to plug leaks. Some clown on TV shows a picture of the statue in Holland of the boy who put his finger in the dike. Stupid.

There is more water in the valley than anyone living – even Armstrong – has ever seen before. It's pounding the Brunkild dike, it's racing down the riverbed and the floodway is at capacity. Something's got to give. The only one of those three things that we mere humans can control is the floodway. Authorities decide it has to take more water, there's no choice. They lift the floodway gates just a little more, in order to raise the water level in the floodway a mere fifteen centimetres. That, spread over the whole floodway is a whole lot of water. Enough, they hope, to make a difference. Enough to save the dike, enough to save the city. But instead of fifteen centimetres, the floodway rises a metre. No one knows why. Water pours into Grande Pointe, sitting just beside the floodway, surrounding most of the houses in the community.

Flood Stop #6.

The next day dawns sunny and bright. It's officially C-Day. The crest rolls through Winnipeg and the Brunkild dike holds.

It's over.

CHAPTER 13

Good-bye

You know what a balloon looks like the day after a party? That's me, all floppy and used up. The party's over. Actually, I don't know why I ever thought this was like a party. It hasn't been any fun for a long time. It's time to take away the eight million sandbags, shovel the muck and sewage out of our houses, tear out our rugs and throw away our furniture. We have to tear apart the Brunkild dike and we only just finished it. Don't need it any more, thanks. We have to haul away those crappy school buses, go back to school and study for exams.

Are you kidding me?

We're old news now. The volunteers have all gone home and the reporters are off to find new stories. Yesterday we were the stars of the show. But that was yesterday.

Gran and I decide that we're going to make Armstrong stay in Winnipeg until we've seen the house. The hospital moved him to a hospice so he has a place to live. There's no point in releasing him if we don't have anywhere to put him. But that means we have to make that first trip all by ourselves. This is his house, more than either Gran's or mine, and it's going to be hard to go there without him. Not to mention the fact that he wants to come home and is furious with us. But even the doctors agree that his health is too fragile for him to be exposed to all that contaminated water. I don't like the sound of that. He doesn't sound fragile when he yells at me over the phone. The doctors say that we all have to be careful about the water because although it started as nice, clean river water, the flood mixed it with sewage, oil, agricultural chemicals and a whole bunch of other nasty stuff. Nice. Gran buys medical gloves to put under our work gloves to protect all the cuts on our hands. She buys lots of garbage bags, too. Other than that, we won't know what we need until we get home. If we still have one. And we can't even look until the water goes down and the military opens the roads. So we wait.

School reopens, since Easthaven is in an area that didn't get flooded. To be truthful, it wasn't actually closed, the Flood Club just didn't go because we had more important things to do. But most kids are back now and it's like the first day after summer vacation. Everybody's comparing stories and there are some whoppers, I can tell you. Not everybody's back, though. There are lots of kids who live in the flood zones who either can't get in or are staying home to help clean up. I'll be one of them soon.

A lot of kids come to tell me they're sorry about Ste. Agathe. There are even a few impromptu gumboot dances, but mostly kids are moving on.

Finally, we get the word that we can go back to Ste. Agathe. Mrs. Taylor says don't be hasty, maybe we should keep on sleeping at their house each night and just work on cleaning up our house by day. We can stay as long as we like, she says, which is really nice. I know what she's really saying is, don't worry if your house is a wreck. You've got friends. That makes me feel scared about what we're going to find.

We're both quiet as we drive in. Armstrong said that when we get there we have to phone him and talk him through the damage. Gran drives into our lane. She stops the truck, takes a big breath and gets out of the truck. I do too. Then she takes my hand, gives it a little squeeze. I squeeze her back.

We still have a house.

The yard is one big mud bath with puddles in places, but mostly the water is gone. I can see how high it got, maybe a metre or so up the front door. The barn is gone. I let go of Gran and run over to look. It's not actually gone, just collapsed. I kick at the boards that used to be the barn door and Gran yells "No, it's dangerous." I know she's right but what about the channel cats?

Gran wants to see inside the house. We go through the back door because the front porch is sagging and we'll probably crash through it. The kitchen's a wreck. There's got to be fifteen centimetres of sludge on the floor, and more sludge sticking to the cupboards and the walls up to that one metre mark. It looks like the water stopped just below the edge of the kitchen counter. We had moved all Gran's flour and sugar and stuff out of the bottom cupboards and onto the kitchen counter so it's all okay. Just the same, Gran looks like she's going to cry, so I say, "At least you can still make cookies." That makes her laugh.

The piano's toast. The paint cans weren't high enough. But because we'd moved all the furniture, the piano is all that's wrecked, well, except for the carpet and the walls.

"It's time to call Armstrong," says Gran. "You talk."

I pull out the cell phone that I talked her into buying. I was pretty sure we'd need it. Armstrong picks up before the first ring is even finished.

"So?" he asks.

I walk through each room, telling him what I see then I go outside and talk him through the yard and the porch. I leave the barn for last.

"Armstrong, I need to go in and see what happened to the catfish."

"Leave them, Finn. We don't have to rush into fixing the barn. You and I can tackle it later."

Armstrong makes me take notes while he tells me who to call and what to ask them to do. Then he asks to talk to Gran. I walk away, because as soon as she starts to talk to Armstrong the tears come, big time.

I kind of want to cry myself. Everyone says we won, we fought the river and won. I don't feel like a winner. Yesterday I was a floodfighter. Today I'm a garbageman.

It's a week before the house is clean enough to let Armstrong come home. He's sure champin' at the bit, as Gran would say. I took pictures of the house and the barn on the new cell phone and took them to the hospice to show him when we visited. We can visit now, because the roads are open. He looked mad. Mad at the river, at the dike – at us? Who knows. He's just Armstrong.

The day we go to get Armstrong is rainy. Gran drives the truck, but I don't go with her. I'll meet her in Winnipeg and ride home with her and Armstrong. For now, I have other plans. Today's the last official Flood Club event and it's going to be big. The principal has organized school buses and we're all going in to Winnipeg. There's going to be a parade. It's for the military. They're leaving and everybody wants to say goodbye. They were so great during the flood, it's the least we can do. I think everybody's sorry to see them go. We're all wearing our red T-shirts and we're going to line up along the convoy route and make a lot of noise. A bunch of kids made signs that say, "Tanks for the memories!" and we have at least ten Canadian flags to wave.

Our buses roll into Winnipeg about an hour before the convoy is supposed to start. We're not allowed to ride in the handicapped bus with Aaron any more, now that the flood is over, so we have to meet up somewhere else. Once we're together, we find the rest of the Flood Club and arrange ourselves along the street – we take up practically a whole block. There's a tonne of people here, even though it's raining. There are little kids and grannies and politicians and office workers – everybody's here. While we wait, we entertain the crowd with some gumboot dancing. I mean, why not? It's our last chance. But when we hear the horns, we get off the street. It's time.

The convoy of military vehicles slowly rolls down the street. The crowd goes wild and I mean it. Everybody's cheering and shouting and waving, even the soldiers. They're honking their horns and waving right back at us. The Flood Club breaks into one of the songs we sang on the sandbagging lines and some of the soldiers who know us join in. And then, you won't believe it. The soldiers that are rolling by – they salute us. All of the red shirts, all of the Flood Club, the soldiers salute us. The girls are crying and I'm yelling so loud I can't hear myself think. It feels so darn good.

I hold on to the high until we get back home. Then the roller coaster comes back down to earth as I watch Armstrong see the damage for the first time, right up close. It's so hard for him to see the mess, especially since those weeks in hospital sure didn't do him any good. He looks weak and shaky, and I wonder if he'll ever be quite the same again. He stands at the wreck of the barn for a long, long time, until he gets all wobbly and has to come inside.

Armstrong says that we'll tackle the barn later. We'll use the tractor to pull away the debris and search for any catfish that are left and after that we can call in help to haul the rest of the wreckage away. But I know he won't be able to do it. He yells as much as ever, but the heart attack and the flood have wrecked his body. He seemed so good in the hospital, but that's not the real world. Here, he can't do much except sit in the kitchen and look out at all the things he wants to do and can't. He can hardly even walk as far as the barn. So I'm just going to have to do it for him.

It's sunny and warm the day I decide to start. Gran has taken Armstrong in to the city for a doctor's appointment, so I have the place to myself. It's probably not smart to try something kind of dangerous when you're alone, but I'm more worried about how Armstrong feels than whether or not some old boards are going to fall on me. I don't really know how to drive the tractor so I put on my old gloves and just pull the broken boards away from the barn. Slow but sure, I make a pile of barn board down near the equipment shed. It's really not that hard because the wood is mostly dry now and it's all so rotted that it's pretty light. I just have to watch out for nails, but even that's not such a big deal because everybody in the Flood Club had to get a tetanus shot before we could work on the sandbag lines. So I'm covered. The plan is to have a big enough pile by the time Armstrong gets home to convince him to let me keep working at it.

And that's just how it goes down. When they get home, Gran gives me this major lecture about how dangerous it was to even try, most of which I don't bother listening to, but Armstrong says I can keep going. It takes a long time, but finally, I get to the shelving.

I bring a stool down to the barn site for Armstrong. It takes him a long time to get there. But his eyes are still good so he scours the debris and tells me where to pull away boards whenever he sees gold. We work like that for two solid days and in the end rescue twelve catfish. Twelve, out of nearly two hundred. A lot are caught in the wreck, but they're smashed to bits. And the rest? Swam out into the Red Sea, I guess.

CHAPTER 14

Cleaning Up

Boring
Boring
Sad
Boring
Hard
Hurts
Boring
Long
Mucky
Tiring
Boring
Makes me mad
Tiring
Dirty
Gross
Ewww, grossest
Hard
Unfair
Depressing

Disgusting
Sad
Lonely

Gran cries a lot. Armstrong's shrinking. He gets smaller and wobblier with every truckload of junk that leaves the yard. If we don't finish soon, there won't be anything left of him.

CHAPTER 15

Happy Birthday

June 1997

It's my birthday. I'm officially fourteen. Mom and Dad used to make a pretty big deal over it. Dad said it was "an important cultural rite of passage" or something but, really, it just means presents. Since we're usually in some other country at this time of year, I've gotten some pretty crazy presents. I think my favourite was the didgeridoo when we were in Australia. One of the elders that lived in the village where we were staying made it for me and tried to teach me how to play, but it was hard. Mom always said it sounded like a wounded moose. Whenever I wanted to drive her crazy I practised. It was good for that. When we were coming home to Canada she said "Thank goodness that awful thing is too big for the plane," but she was so wrong! At the airport, they have a special place for wrapping up didgeridoos and they let you send it right through. Mom was very annoyed with the airlines.

I haven't said anything about my birthday. I mean, I think Gran knows (she's my Gran and they always know stuff like that), and I'm pretty sure there's a monster cake planned, but other than that, nobody feels like partying much. That's okay by me. It's not like I'm a little kid or anything. And everything's kind of depressing right now.

The porch is fixed, the carpet's gone, the kitchen cupboards have been pulled out and so have all the lower interior walls. The basement's dry and the sludge has been shovelled out. The house looks all torn apart, but the inspector says it's safe for now. It's a really old house so he wants us to check the wiring before we put new walls up and electricians are pretty busy these days. We have to wait. So we moved the furniture back downstairs and we're going to pretend everything's okay even if we don't have walls.

Gran's even thinking about planting a late garden, now that the ground has dried up. She says that crops are spectacular the year after a flood and she doesn't want to miss that.

But it's still depressing.

Gran makes my favourite breakfast, but she doesn't say happy birthday. She's so funny. I mean, I know there's a cake in the cupboard. Armstrong talks about going fishing. He talks about it a lot. I ask Gran if she'll drive me to Easthaven so I can hang with my friends and when she says no, that's when I know something's up. She never says no. So I have to pretend to be all surprised when Mrs. Taylor comes driving up the lane and everybody piles out of the van. It's great, though.

First off, everybody goes to say hi to Armstrong. It's like he's some kind of royalty now because he was still a floodfighter when he was ninety-four. He really likes the attention, but he keeps looking at the door, which makes me wonder. I don't have to wonder for long.

You are not going to believe this. A truck rolls up the lane. That's nothing new, we've had a million trucks up our lane. But this one has a trailer, and on the trailer is — wait for it — an ATV. I'm not kidding. A 4X4 All Terrain Vehicle, fuel-injected 475 cc with an automatic clutch. It's red. Front and back racks. It is sooo sweet.

I just stare. Then Gran says, "Don't get too excited, Finn, it stays on the farm. It's actually for Armstrong, so he can get around the property a little better. But now that you're fourteen, you can drive it."

Aaron says, "Hey buddy, now I'm not the only one with wheels." I grin. I can't stop grinning. The driver is unloading the ATV and we crowd around. Gran nods and I climb up on the seat. She's not giving me the keys yet, but just sitting up there feels good.

"Your turn, Armstrong." We help him up. He's still wobbly, but his face looks more alive than it has for a while. I whisper to Gran, "Are you sure about this?" She whispers back, "The doctor said okay, but he can't go off the property. When we get the barn rebuilt, it will let him go back and forth on his own."

This is so cool. We all take turns sitting on it and I can't wait to try it out. But for now, we have cake. Then there's another surprise, and not just for me.

"Okay everybody," says Clara. "Consider yourselves booked on June 21. I've entered us in the teen talent competition at the Red River Ex."

"You did what?" shrieks Jane.

"'Starring You at the Ex.' The teen talent competition. We'll be fantastic!"

"What exactly is our talent?" asks Aaron drily. "I know my chair is pretty hot, and now Finn's got some great wheels, but I don't know what the rest of you are going to show off."

"Oh, for heaven's sake," says Clara. "Don't you get it? We're going to do our gumboot dance. We already have our costumes and everything."

Another long silence.

"How do you come up with this stuff?" asks Roy, shaking his head.

Good question. But I like it. Putting my red shirt back on, having some fun. What's wrong with that?

"I'm in," I say. Then I stick out my fist. "Floodfighters!" Clara grins and puts her hand on mine. "Floodfighters!" Aaron rolls his eyes and Roy groans, but five seconds later everybody else piles hands. "Floodfighters!!"

Armstrong bursts out laughing for the first time in forever.

CHAPTER 16

The Channel Cat

Tooling around on the Red Ripper is wicked. That's what we're calling the ATV, after one of Armstrong's favourite fishing lures. I can go on back roads all the way to Easthaven, so now I don't have to ask Gran to take me all the time. Even Armstrong's doing okay on the Ripper, as long as we help him get on and off. Once he's on, he's off. If you know what I mean.

The Saturday before the Ex I get up and Armstrong's making hot dogs. For breakfast? Gross. It turns out they're not for eating.

"Today's the day, Finn," says Armstrong. "We're going fishing."

All right! I was beginning to think his fishing days would be over before mine even started.

"Are those for fishing?" I ask. I pull up his stool to the counter to watch.

Armstrong cuts the wieners into pieces then throws them into a baggie. Then he dumps in two packages of cherry Kool-Aid, closes the bag and does a shake-and-bake thing. "Catfish love the colour red. And they don't care what they eat. So these make great bait." I snort. Cold wieners sound like a perfect meal for a bottom-feeder. When he's done I collect his fishing gear and his stool. Then I help him up onto the Ripper. It's a one-seater (Gran wanted something small), so I have to walk along beside him down to the riverbank. Run, actually, because he's a crazy driver. Getting down to the river is kind of hard for him. It's not like the bank is that far down, but when he's off the ATV he's doesn't do so good.

He gets settled on his stool and shows me how to set the bait. He goes on and on about different kinds of lures and what kind of bait works the best (besides the cut-up wieners rolled in Kool-Aid). He points out his favourite spots, the deep quiet places snugged up by deadfall where the catfish like to rest, and I cast the line. I have to do it a couple of times because my aim's not very good yet. Finally, Armstrong approves of where the line drops and we wait. And wait.

Then there's a tug. Not a very big one, but it's still a surprise. I hold tight to the rod and Armstrong talks me through the fight, telling me how long to let the fish run and when to reel it closer. It seems to go on for a long time before I actually see the fish. It's still under the surface so there isn't any splashing, but I see it and feel it writhe as it tries to dislodge the hook. Armstrong hands me the net. He takes the rod just for a minute because that's all he can do, but it's enough so that I'm able to reach out and net the fish. Armstrong drops the rod and we take a look at it.

"A very respectable catfish," pronounces Armstrong, but I can see he's not very excited about it. I don't know, it looks pretty big to me. Armstrong shows me how to remove the hook, then I lower the fish, still in the net, back into the water. Armstrong tells me how to stroke the fish, gently moving it backwards and forwards in the water to help the gills start working again. And when the fish shows some life, I let it go.

"Again," instructs Armstrong, and I set new bait. This time, he has me pick where I want the line to go. I try to imagine where I would want to be if I was a channel cat. I point, Armstrong approves and I make my cast. Like before, it takes a couple of tries to get my line over there, but I do. And we wait.

This time everything's different. The jerk on the line practically pulls me into the water. I'm concentrating on how to hang on to it and listen to Armstrong's instructions at the same time. I can feel the power quivering along the line, and I know this isn't just a catfish — it's a true channel cat. He pulls and I let him go. I reel him in, but can only go so far until he powers away. I reel him in again. Back and forth we go. I understand now what Peter meant about the tug of war. Back and forth. Fight. Release. Fight.

I'm winning, at least I think I am. If I didn't have all those muscles from sandbagging I don't know if I could keep up the pressure. The fight goes on and on. Somehow I get the feeling that the channel cat is toying with me, that he's not really tired, he just wants to test me. I keep working, reel in, power away. Each time the channel cat gets closer to the surface. Reel in, power away. And then I see him.

He's monstrous, maybe a metre long and at least thirteen kilos, and he's thrashing about like crazy. I think he's angry now. I don't think he meant to let me bring him this high. He's just below the surface of the water so I can see him clearly, and he's an ugly son of a gun. His dorsal fin is sticking straight up out of the water. That's the part I saw before when I was in Bruce's

Zodiac. There are four long whiskery things sticking out from his chin, at least, from where there would be a chin if he had one. But it's the two long barbs that grow out from each side of his huge mouth that grab my attention. I've never seen anything so gross. He rises up to the top and that mouth opens real wide and, for a second, I think his bulging eyes are staring right into mine. Then the line snaps and he's gone.

I'm so startled that I fall right on my backside and that's when I hear applause behind me. I scramble up and spin around and see Peter standing behind me. Even Armstrong is surprised to see him, I can tell from his face.

"Well done, Finn!" says Peter, who is still clapping his hands. "You are officially a channel cat fisherman now!"

Armstrong looks troubled. "What are you doing here, Peter?" he asks with concern in his voice. "The flood is over, isn't it?"

"Of course it is," replies Peter. "I came to say goodbye."

"You're not coming back?" I ask.

"Yes, I'll be back. But Armstrong won't."

My face goes white. What is that supposed to mean?

"I brought you a gift." Peter hands Armstrong a tiny carved channel cat. It's wicked. It looks exactly like the channel cat I just fought, only small.

"Don't worry about the ones that were lost," Peter says. "They will find their own way, just as all channel cats do. Just as we do." Peter smiles at Armstrong.

The two old friends clasp hands. If I didn't know better, I'd say that Armstrong's transparent hand looks more ghostly than Peter's.

I feel a little frantic. Sure, Peter can tell the future when it comes to floods, but what the heck does he know about my great-grandfather? "The doctor says he's fine!"

"Finn, it's all right," says Armstrong. He reaches out his hand to me, but I back away. I don't want to be part of this.

I can't believe what I'm hearing. Armstrong can't die. I'm just getting to know him. And I don't want his secret. It's too big for me to manage.

"I'm not ready!"

Armstrong doesn't agree. "Don't worry, Finn. Do you think any of the Armstrongs were ready for something like this? It's your turn, and you'll manage, just as we all have. Anyway, I'm not going anywhere yet."

"You're sure?" I won't cry in front of him, I won't.

"I'm pretty sure it won't be today," he replies drily. "But soon; I am ninety-four."

Peter chuckles then says, "Finn, you and I will work something out. Don't worry." He and Armstrong share one last look then he turns around and starts walking down the riverbank.

I try to keep my eyes on him but all of a sudden he's not there. Maybe I blinked. All I know for sure is that he doesn't think we're done with each other.

Armstrong tells me to bundle up the gear and help him up the bank. He's giving orders just as if nothing happened. And I do everything he says because I like it better that way. Really, I do. Him being in charge and me taking orders. I don't want it to be my turn.

But just like the flood, I guess I don't have a choice.

CHAPTER 17

The Red River Ex

Mrs. Taylor drives us all to the exhibition grounds. I'm kind of stoked. I mean, who doesn't like a fair? And it feels good to be back in my red T-shirt. The talent show isn't until the afternoon, so we have lots of time to explore. First stop is the horse show. I've never seen anything like it. The riders are all acrobats and they do back flips on and off horses that are galloping around a ring. They juggle fire while they're standing on horseback, they even ride underneath the horses. I'd like to stay but the girls want to go to Extreme Dog Grooming. Are you kidding me? Who wants to see a poodle painted purple?

Finally we get to the midway. This is kind of hard. Aaron isn't allowed to go on a lot of the rides. He says it's okay and makes all the rest of us buy passes. It's hard to say no, because man, it's a great midway. They've got the Mega Drop and the Fireball, the Blitzer roller coaster and the Orbitor, even Pharaoh's Fury. Hey, I'm going to Egypt after all! And it turns out Aaron's not doing so badly himself. When we get off the Zipper there are some girls we don't know talking to him. As we get up close we can hear them.

"Aren't you the guy that was on TV, you know, during the flood? They said you could throw more sandbags than anybody!" Ewwww. If they ask to see his muscles I'll barf.

After that he comes with us on some of the rides that can take the chair, like the haunted mansion and the video funhouse. And we eat and eat and eat. Man, I love a good fair.

Finally it's time for the talent contest, which is probably good because, after all I've eaten, if I go on any more rides I might really barf. We sign in backstage and find the rest of the red shirts. I didn't tell you this before, but just like the Flood Club, Clara's idea kind of went cosmic. Once word got out that we were going to do one last gumboot dance, the rest of the Flood Club wanted in. We said sure, but then the organizers said we could only have thirty people or the stage would collapse. So it had to be first come, first served. Hazel kept the sign-up sheet so we would know who the first people on the list were. Fred's one of them. Who'd have thought? But we have way more than thirty people on our list.

We're all wearing our red T-shirts, our rubber boots, and dollar store hard hats. We decide to wear our work gloves too because they're part of the floodfighter uniform. When it's our turn, we file out onto the stage. Everybody cheers. We're kind of famous now, you know. Gran and even Armstrong are in the crowd, and Mr. and Mrs. Taylor, and Clara's mom, and Barb and Bert and the twins, and Mrs. St. Pierre and Ned, and the principal...everybody, really. We've been practising in the school gym and we have some really wicked rhythms now.

I start with the chant.

HEE MAHLALELA

HAMBH' UYO SEBENZA
HEE MAHLALELA
HAMBH' UYO SEBENZA

We all start slapping our boots. Then we add the hand-clapping. We get into a simple kick-stomp. Then it gets faster. We add some moves. I do a solo. The girls do some kick-slaps. Aaron does a wheelchair solo and the crowd goes wild. We get faster and faster until we can't get any faster, and that's when we go cosmic.

Remember that list? As if we were going to say *no, you can't* come to any of the Flood Club. No way. All the Ex said was that they couldn't be on the stage. So just when we're going crazy fast, I start the chant again only this time it's not just me. Everybody, and I mean *everybody*, starts chanting with me. And red shirts are everywhere, behind the audience, on both sides of the audience, all through the audience and they stomp their way to the front and we're on the stage and they're just in front of us on the ground, and we're chanting and we're clapping and we're stomping and it's epic. The most epic epic *ever*.

We win.

Duh.

That night I go home with Aaron for a sleepover. It feels kind of natural to sleep on his floor now. When he turns out the light and it's really dark I tell him my news.

"My mom and dad have been pretty freaked out by all this," I start.

"No doubt."

"So, it looks like I'm not leaving."

"What?!"

"Yeah, they're worried about Gran and Armstrong and getting the house repaired and everything, so they made this deal with the university. When they finish in Russia they'll teach at the University of Manitoba, instead of UBC. We're going to live here."

"That is totally awesome, man. But what about Egypt? You were pretty stoked about that."

"Yeah, well, not so much any more. I mean, this thing with Peter…"

"Yeah, I get it."

We're quiet for a bit.

"You know, Finn?" says Aaron. "I'm not an Armstrong or anything, but I don't mind helping with that. I mean, I won't tell anybody and if it gets weirder or anything, I can cover for you."

It would be nice not to have to keep this secret from at least somebody. So I say sure.

More quiet.

"Clara's going be happy," he says slyly.

"Whatever," I say. Aaron laughs.

Quiet.

"Hey, Finn?"

"Yeah?"

"What does that chant mean anyway?"

"It means 'Loafer go and work.'"

We laugh so hard Mr. Taylor has to bang on the wall.

And that's my story. Believe it or not.
I couldn't hold back the flood, even though I really tried.
Maybe I wasn't supposed to.

By the way, if you ever happen to find a wooden catfish
swimming through the prairie grass,
will you take it back to the Red River where it belongs?
Thanks.

Signed,
Finn Armstrong

Author's Notes

The disastrous flood of 1997 was called the Flood of the Century. But it wasn't a surprise, and it could happen again. Just as Ned explains in geography class, flooding is part of the character of the Red River. Learning to live with the natural flow of the river means enjoying the good and preparing for the bad. The people of the Red River Valley truly are special in their ability to do just that. Like channel cats, they have learned the secrets of the river and use that knowledge to protect themselves, while still allowing the river to flow naturally around them.

Truth or Fiction?

This book, like all of the books in the *Disaster Strikes!* series, is historical fiction. Some of the events and the characters are real and others come from my imagination. Truth or fiction – which is which?

There were many real heroes of the 1997 flood. Alf Warkentin, Ron Richardson and Don Kuryk are all real people who played very important roles in the flood, just as they do in this book. But many of the other characters, such as Finn and his friends in the Flood Club, come from my imagination.

The flooding of Ste. Agathe and Grande Pointe really happened. Both events were totally unexpected, as is the case with so many disasters. Flooding was probably going to happen, but not in those two places. The Brunkild Dike was real too, thanks to Mr. Richardson and Mr. Kuryk and the hundreds of people who helped do the impossible. And *Starring You at the Ex* at the

Red River Exhibition happens every year in June, but whether or not the Flood Club would have had a chance at winning with their gumboot dance, you'll have to decide for yourself!

The River That Runs Backwards

The Red River is eight hundred and eighty-five kilometres long and flows across the bed of the ancient glacial Lake Agassiz. As the ice age glaciers melted, the lake formed. It was bigger than all the Great Lakes combined and held more water than all of the lakes in the world today. And it was that ancient glacier that determined the direction the river flows, the direction that is the cause for all the trouble.

Why doesn't the river run from Lake Winnipeg south to the United States? The glaciers in the north were heavy. And when something heavy sits on the earth for a very long time the earth sinks under the weight. So the land in the north is lower than the land in the south and just like Finn said, the river runs *down*.

But now that the glaciers are gone, the earth is starting to tilt back. It won't be for thousands of years, but some day the Red River might just change direction and give our descendents a flood-free future.

The Floodway

The Red River floodway is recognized as one of the world's greatest engineering marvels. After the terrible damage done by the flood of 1950, Manitoba Premier "Duff" Roblin came up with the idea of the floodway. People thought he was crazy and the project was named "Roblin's Folly." But the Premier

knew it was needed, so he put his whole career on the line to get it built. It took six years to build and at the time was the second largest earthmoving project in the world, next only to the Panama Canal.

The floodway cost $63 million to build and has already saved $32 billion in flood damages. It's not called "Roblin's Folly" any more! Now it's known as "Duff's Ditch". And it's a really BIG ditch!

For information on the floodway and some cool pictures of the construction process, check out: www.floodwayauthority.mb.ca.

The Military

It was called Operation Assistance, and up until that time was the biggest peacetime military operation Canada had ever mounted. It was no wonder Finn thought Winnipeg felt like a war zone. It was the largest military operation since the war in Korea, with more than eight thousand troops from the army, the navy and air force involved.

1997 was a period of time when the public had some negative feelings about the military and the work they were doing in Africa. The help the soldiers provided during the flood changed all that, as people got to see up close how hard all the soldiers worked.

For a great video of the military in action in the flood zone, go to YouTube and search for "Red River Flood – Military Aid."

Channel Cats

"Rude, mean bullies who like a knockdown fight, one so bad

it leaves everybody bruised..."

That's how fishers describe channel cats. And yet, like Peter and Armstrong, fishers come to fight with the Red River channel cats from all over North America. Red River cats average seven to ten kilograms, but monsters over eighteen kilograms are caught every year. They are considered to be trophy fish. Lots of fishers enter contests to see who can catch the biggest one.

In Winnipeg, kids like Finn and Aaron can go to Fish Camp, a summer camp for young fishers. Now that would be an adventure!

Gumboot Dancing

Gumboot dancing originated in the gold mines of South Africa. As Finn says in chapter seven, the mines were often flooded, and the barefoot workers began to get foot ulcers and diseases from the water. Rather than drain the mines, the bosses decided it was cheaper just to get the workers rubber boots. They added work overalls and hard hats to create a uniform. This was a problem for the miners, who traditionally used their clothing to show their ethnic background. In the uniform, everyone looked the same.

Another problem was that the mines were very dark and working conditions were harsh. The men were chained to their workstations, could not see one another and were not allowed to speak, sometimes for months at a time. In desperation, the workers began to tap out the rhythms of their traditional songs as a way of identifying themselves. The rhythms expanded to become a form of communication between workers, one that the guards did not understand. As

gumboot dancing became more popular, mining companies began to encourage it and had the workers entertain investors in order to show how happy their employees were. Little did they know that the labourers were actually making fun of them in public!

There are some great videos of gumboot dancing on YouTube; just search for "gumboot dance."

Cribbage

Finn says that cribbage is from "like, the Dark Ages", but it isn't quite that old. In the early seventeenth century, the English poet, Sir James Suckling, created a version of the game called noddy. Noddy has disappeared, but cribbage remains one of the most popular games in the world. It is the official game of American submariners, and the personal crib board of World War II Medal of Honor Recipient, Dick O'Kane, is always carried on the oldest active submarine in the American fleet. If the submarine is decommissioned, the crib board is moved to the next oldest submarine.

The object of the game is to group cards together in patterns that will gain points. Groups that add up to fifteen are particularly important. Two important elements of the game are the crib and the scoreboard. The crib is a small group of cards that is set aside until the end of the hand and can gain extra points for the dealer. The scoreboard is usually made of a piece of wood drilled with tiny holes. Small wooden (today we often use plastic or metal) pegs are stuck in the holes as points are counted.

I decided to add cribbage to the story because it's a game that spans generations. It would be very common for a great-grandfather to play it with a great-grandson, and for families to play the game together. I also thought the idea of the wooden crib board fit nicely with Peter's carving. In our house, we have two handmade crib boards made by my father-in-law. One is a traditional tabletop version, and the other is giant-sized. It has its own legs and looks like a narrow table that sits between the players. Cribbage is a popular game in our family and we have some very serious players!

Flood Trivia

- When the flood crested in Winnipeg, there was enough water flowing to fill an Olympic-sized pool every second.
- One of the benefits of the flood was a virtually bug-free summer. The water washed away most of the mosquito larvae.
- Remember how Finn complained about the cleanup? It was hard to find people to take apart the dikes and get rid of the millions of sandbags so, in the end, the city of Winnipeg had to pay a private company half a million dollars to do the job.
- Don Kuryk from the Manitoba Highways Department was the man who got the Brunkild Dike built in time. In thanks, the Armed Forces gave him a Distinguished Service Medal.

The Flood: By the Numbers

- $3.5 billion: damage to property
- 28,000: number of people evacuated from their homes
- 600,000 cubic metres: amount of clay excavated to build city dikes
- 8,100,000: number of sandbags used in Winnipeg alone
- 1,000: number of sandbags filled each hour by a Sandbagger machine with a crew of 50
- 77,000: number of volunteers
- 600: number of journalists who covered the flood, from Canada and abroad
- 77%: estimated percentage of Winnipeggers who watched *Plugged In!*
- $63 million: original cost of the floodway, completed in 1968
- $32 billion: amount saved by the floodway, through avoided flood damage

Acknowledgements

My sincere thanks go to my friends at Coteau Books, who first came up with the idea for this series and have wholeheartedly supported it ever since. It was a pleasure to work with my editor, Kathryn Cole; I thank you for the commas! On a technical note, the Gumboot Song that the Flood Club sings at the Ex (and the English translation) is from the *World Arts West Dance Style Viewer's Guide* at www.worldartswest.org.

As always, tight hugs to my family who continue to support and encourage this writing habit of mine.

 **PENNY DRAPER** is an author, a bookseller and a storyteller who lives in Victoria, BC. Originally from Toronto, she received a degree in literature from Trinity College, University of Toronto, and attended the Storytellers' School of Toronto. For many years, Penny shared tales as a professional storyteller at schools, libraries, conferences and festivals as well as on radio and television. She has told stories in an Arabian harem and from inside a bear's belly – but that is a story in itself.

Penny's books have been nominated for numerous awards in Canada and the United States. They have been honoured with the Victoria Book Prize, the Moonbeam Award Gold Medal and the Chocolate Lily Readers' Choice Award (runner-up). *Red River Raging* is part of the Coteau Books *Disaster Strikes!* series. The series also includes Penny's *Terror at Turtle Mountain*, *Peril at Pier Nine*, *Graveyard of the Sea*, *A Terrible Roar of Water*, *Ice Storm* and *Day of the Cyclone*.

MIX

Paper from
responsible sources

FSC® C016245

www.fsc.org

 ENVIRONMENTAL BENEFITS STATEMENT

Coteau Books saved the following resources by printing the pages of this book on chlorine free paper made with 100% post-consumer waste.

TREES	WATER	ENERGY	SOLID WASTE	GREENHOUSE GASES
12	5,553	5	371	1,024
FULLY GROWN	GALLONS	MILLION BTUs	POUNDS	POUNDS

 Environmental impact estimates were made using the Environmental Paper Network Paper Calculator 3.2. For more information visit www.papercalculator.org.